Why could he not rise?

He remembered the battle—he could see it all now in patterns of black and white. Violence had its own aura, as did so many things in the world, a combination of sight and smell. People smelled different when angry or afraid.

He'd fought at Barta's side as he always had and always would, and taken a number of wounds. They didn't matter, only her welfare mattered, and his presence at her side.

For him, battle felt like a game, a violent one. So long as Barta remained with him and protected, he cared little what else happened, even to him. He existed to be with her, to protect her—nothing more.

But now she arose from the place where they'd both gone down—where he'd thrown his body in defense of hers—and he could not follow.

For the first time in his life he could not follow.

Oh, unbearable agony. For, faintly, he could still feel her, smell her tears, sense her touch. He could feel her starting to move away from him, feel her spirit tug at his. They were bound together, always had been, by a silver cord stronger than leather and more potent than magic.

Love.

Do not leave me here, Mistress. I cannot rise. I cannot follow you.

Like hers, his spirit howled at the sky.

Praise for Laura Strickland

Laura Strickland's novella *FORGED BY LOVE* won first place in the short historical category of the International Digital Awards.

~*~

"The world building is phenomenal."

~Daysie W. at My Book Addiction and More

~*~

"Laura Strickland creates a world that not only draws you in, but she incorporates it…seamlessly. …the kind of book that keeps you awake well into the wee hours, and sighing with satisfaction when you've finished the very last page."

~Nicole McCaffrey, author

~*~

"As I read I became so involved with the story, I found it difficult to put down the book. …Definitely …an author to watch."

~Dandelion at Long & Short Reviews

Loyal and True

by

Laura Strickland

Hearts of Caledonia, Book One

Loyal and True

Cover Art by *Diana Carlile*

The Wild Rose Press, Inc.
PO Box 708
Adams Basin, NY 14410-0708
Visit us at www.thewildrosepress.com

Publishing History
First Fantasy Rose Edition, 2018
Print ISBN 978-1-5092-1856-1
Digital ISBN 978-1-5092-1857-8

Hearts of Caledonia, Book One
Published in the United States of America

Dedication

For Mac, Tug, Shannon, Jessie, and especially Mara,
who taught me so much about
the unbreakable bonds of love.

Other Books by Laura Strickland
available from The Wild Rose Press, Inc.

A word about the Picts and the Caledonii

Dear Reader,

Not a great deal is known about the Picts, certainly not as much as we might wish. They left few written records, which makes research for even a work of romantic fiction challenging. One thing we do know is that they did not call themselves "Picts." That appellation was leveled by the Romans and stemmed from the pictures (tattoos) they wore on their skin, so numerous they were often referred to as "blue men."

At the time of my story, Celtic clans had moved into western Scotland from Ireland and settled the kingdom of Dal Riada. The north and east of Scotland, a vast territory, was still controlled by tribes loosely gathered under the name "Caledonii." Beneath this name there existed sub-tribes, and I have called mine the "Epidii." Predictably, conflict arose between the Gaels and the Caledonii, who contested for land. Later, as legend has it, they would be united under Kenneth MacAlpin, but before then a considerable amount of fighting and displacement must have ensued.

The language of the Picts/Caledonii has not survived except in place names and some given names inscribed on stones. Research tells us it was closely related to ancient Welsh, and I have chosen to give my characters names with an ancient Briton/Welsh flavor. Since this is in fact a work of romantic fiction, I hope you will join me in imagining the details of Caledonian life, including what they may have called one another—and their hounds.

Caledonian hearts are loyal and true.
Caledonian hearts are valiant and wise.
Caledonian hearts are noble and blessed.

Chapter One

The region of Pitlochry, Scotland, 754 AD

She could not breathe. Oh, dear goddess, why couldn't she breathe?

Flat on her back and disoriented, Barta stared upward. A sharp crescent moon hung in the black vault of the sky like a shard of ice, pinned stark against the darkness—the first thing she saw when she opened her eyes. She blinked at it, wondering where she lay and just how she had come here. Deep silence drummed in her ears, and a terrible, great weight pressed down on her chest, making her fight desperately to inhale.

What did she recall? With her eyes fixed on that wicked, deadly moon, she groped mentally for the pieces of reality. There had been a raid. She herself had precipitated it and had attacked, accompanied by several companions. She'd thought they could do a nighttime hit-and-run on the Gaels who'd been so insistent about pushing into their territory all season long. Others among her tribe's warriors had disagreed. She strove to remember the course of things beyond that and failed. She recalled only the crash of weapons, the screams of ponies and men, and the terror caused by the Gaels' chariots, which they used like mobile weapons.

Now all lay still—far too still to bode well for

Barta and her fellow tribesmen. The moon—not yet risen when she and her companions left home with their spears on their shoulders—hung far to the west. Time had passed, too much time. Why couldn't she recall?

A strange and terrifying thought occurred: her headlong impetuosity, for which her father ceaselessly faulted her, might have caught up with her at last. He'd long insisted death must come for her before her time and that it stalked her even more surely than it did other Epidii warriors. She might be dead. Was that why she had to fight so hard to breathe?

She'd often declared she didn't fear death or the subsequent flight over land and water to the afterlife. Had that been a lie? She certainly tasted terror now in the back of her throat and knew herself unprepared to leave this wild, dangerous world with all its beauties, or this land for which she'd been so willing to fight.

Barta blinked at the moon again and focused on sensation. Not dead, no—she could feel far too much: pain from a half-score of wounds and the dreadful struggle to drag breath into her lungs. Her heartbeat, so strong it shook her body. This terrible weight pressing down on her and a persistent, wet warmth. The smell of…

Blood.

Ah, goddess, she lay here soaked by it!

That knowledge got her moving, scrambling up, fighting against her panic and the pain in every limb. She slid with difficulty out from under the mighty weight that pinned her and fought her way to her feet, where a terrible sight met her eyes.

Destruction spread around her in a wide swath. Here a downed pennant, there a smashed chariot. The bodies of the fallen, both Epidii and Gael, sprawled everywhere. The living—gone. Impossible to tell in this stark, uncertain light how long ago the skirmish had ended or who had won. She must have been left for dead beneath...

She looked, blinked, and stared in disbelief. Her heart seized in her chest.

No. Goddess no, not that. Not...

For an instant her mind refused to accept the evidence before her eyes. But yes, if she, Barta lay here, Loyal would be here also. She should have remembered that at once, should have thought of him as soon as she opened her eyes. Because he was the embodiment of his name, had been from his first breath right up to his very—

Last.

No, by the hart and hind, no. He must merely lie injured—knocked down senseless like Barta herself. He'd done what any good war hound should and laid his body over hers in an act of protection.

A final act.

But he couldn't be dead. She wouldn't allow it. The goddess, merciful and beautiful, wouldn't allow it. He merely slept.

With a cry of distress, Barta fell to her knees beside the deerhound's sprawled form and placed her hands in his fur. He lay on his side with his long legs outstretched, head drawn back in what looked like a strain of agony. Others of their fallen lay around him, for the heart of the fight had taken place here. Barta began to remember it now, the chariots—accursed weapons on wheels—had herded the Epidii like beasts, and the Gaels had cut them apart. Trapped. A knot of

Epidii caught just here fighting desperately.

Loyal, at Barta's side as always, snarling, leaping to her defense, throwing himself between Barta and the weapons of her opponents. That did not mean he now lay dead. They'd fought together so many times and always survived.

Why did she not remember him falling?

The answer came to her even as she ran her palms across his fur. Still warm. Yes, he had to be alive. But her hands came away drenched with his blood.

She gazed at her palms by the cruel light of the glittering moon. Loyal's blood covered them. Yet it took her an instant to realize the truth: his head had been drawn back not in agony but so some Gaelic warrior—now dead or departed—might slit his throat.

A cry of despair escaped her, and she collapsed over the hound's body, denial pounding through her. She could smell the beloved scent of his still-warm fur along with his blood—ripe, sharp, and primal.

Her mind told her no one, not even a courageous war hound full of strength, could survive such a wound. Her heart and her lips cried out for him.

Loyal—do not leave me. You cannot! How can I go on if you leave me? Come back...please come back to me!

****

Wild with pain, Barta cried into the darkness and received no response. The limbs beneath her hands did not stir; the hound did not strive to rise to her call. Slowly, heart burst and aching, Barta dragged herself to her feet.

The battlefield, deserted except for the dead, glittered with blood and abandoned weapons. Two of

Barta's tribe mates, both staring sightlessly at the moon, lay close by. Barta, who herself bled from several places, eyed their wounds and gulped back another sob. Oh, what had she done?

And what to do now? At first light, the crows would come and begin their work. She did not want to leave her companions—and especially Loyal—here for them to pillage. She wanted to carry him home and assail him with honor, but doubted she could. The great hound weighed more than she did, and she alone appeared to have survived the battle.

Alone.

She had never felt more alone than she did at that moment. She cried out to the goddess again in a wail of pain that split the night.

"Help me! I cannot leave him here. I will not."

Unnatural strength came and filled her, fueled by her agony. She bent and attempted to gather the great hound into her arms. His head lolled and revealed his terrible wound.

Another sob tore from her. Though every muscle quivered, she could not succeed in lifting him, not even with the goddess's assistance. She must leave him here. Unless...

One of her fellows, like her, survived.

She abandoned the hound and went about from man to man, stooping and steadily weeping harder. Six men lay nearby, close friends all, and every one dead. She had not meant it to end like this—it had been a simple act of defiance on her part, intended to discourage the Gaels from encroaching further onto Epidii land. Barta's idea, all hers. By the goddess, she had persuaded them. To their deaths.

5

A quick blow, she had thought to strike, hitting from out of the dark at an unprepared scouting band. But the Gaels had proved more in number than expected and had fought back hard. She now recalled seeing their leader—a man with flying, yellow hair—rallying his men and using those accursed chariots to best effect, cutting the Epidii apart.

Now, though, every living soul had departed. That didn't mean the Gaels would not return—several of their dead still lay here on the bloodied ground, and experience told her they would not neglect them for long.

She had to get away from here at once. But how to leave her friends…and Loyal?

She tried to think how long it would take her to get home and back again with the help needed to fetch her dead. She could not be sure how far off the Gaels' main encampment might lie, but it should take them considerable time to return.

She fell to her knees again and twined her arms about her hound, planting one palm against his great chest, where she'd always been able to feel his heartbeat.

Stilled now.

She kissed his muzzle and tasted his blood on her lips. She wailed again in despair, heedless of her danger should the retreating Gaels hear. Let them return and slay her; her heart already lay here on the ground.

She'd been no more than seventeen when her father's bitch, Bright, had a new litter.

"Choose one for yourself," Father told Barta. That had been before his injury on the field, back when he still retained his strength and vigor. "The hounds are always following after you anyway, and if you intend going into battle like a son rather than a daughter, you will need a good hound at your side."

It had been easy to choose. Eight pups had Bright whelped, all brindle-gray like her. They'd played, climbed, and tumbled over each other in the way of pups everywhere—all but one who focused on Barta with bright hazel eyes and tottered after her whenever she took a step.

Father had laughed. "That's the one, Daughter. A male, and he's going to be big and strong, judging by the size of those paws. You could do worse."

Barta already knew that. The pup had chosen her rather than the other way round.

She'd taken days to decide on a name for him. Even that had come naturally when folk saw him trotting after her around the settlement, each of them saying with a smile, "Well, Barta, he looks to prove loyal."

Loyal he'd been for every day of the four years since. They'd walked together, trained and played together, eaten their meals and slept together. Inseparable.

Until now.

Tears streamed down her face, making the hound's body blur before her eyes. "Oh, Loyal, how can I leave you when you've never, ever left me?"

Yet he'd given his life in her defense. Could she turn around and throw that gift away by letting the Gaels return and catch her here?

She must go. And she could not take him with her.

Again she kissed him, her tears mingling with his blood, again got to her feet, moving like an old woman.

She found her knife—half under Loyal's body—and rifled the corpses of her friends for their weapons. Weaponry was scarce and too valuable to lose.

Just like these lives, her heart whispered to her.

The Gaels had already stolen enough. Still it took many long moments before she turned her back and slipped away into the consuming darkness.

****

Loyal!

He lay enfolded in darkness, floating like a bark on a vast ocean, peaceful enough until he heard that cry of agony and—as he had all his life—strove to respond. He must go to her when she called him. His very existence revolved around that truth. His mistress was his sun, his moon, his reason for drawing breath. No thought for himself could ever intrude ahead of a thought of her.

And she called him. More, she needed him. He must respond.

Why could he not rise?

He remembered the battle—he could see it all now in patterns of black and white. Violence had its own aura, as did so many things in the world, a combination of sight and smell. People smelled different when angry or afraid.

He'd fought at Barta's side as he always had and always would, and taken a number of wounds. They didn't matter, only her welfare mattered, and his presence at her side.

For him, battle felt like a game, a violent one. So long as Barta remained with him and protected, he cared little what else happened, even to him. He existed to be with her, to protect her—nothing more.

But now she arose from the place where they'd both gone down—where he'd thrown his body in defense of hers—and he could not follow.

For the first time in his life he could not follow.

Oh, unbearable agony. For, faintly, he could still feel her, smell her tears, sense her touch. He could feel her starting to move away from him, feel her spirit tug at his. They were bound together, always had been, by a silver cord stronger than leather and more potent than magic.

Love.

Do not leave me here, Mistress. I cannot rise. I cannot follow you.

Like hers, his spirit howled at the sky.

Chapter Two

"You foolish girl! Heedless, accursed girl! How dare you go behind my back—and behind your brother's—to launch a raid? What were you thinking, taking so much upon yourself? And only see what has come of it."

Barta's father raged as she stood before him in the dim hut, hollered like a man gone mad. It had not been easy for her to come creeping in and confess the truth; only the need to go collect their dead had lent her the raw courage.

She could see by the fire in her father's eyes that he wanted to strike her. Good thing perhaps that he could not—crippled as he was, he struggled even to rise. Though he still led their tribe—among the most southern of the Caledonii—he did so from a pallet hoisted by his men, unable to enter battle, and sorely frustrated.

Now his broad face creased with worry and pain, and the rest of the family, ranged around him, stared in silent horror.

"How many dead?" Radoc roared. "Say that to me again!"

Somehow, Barta raised her gaze to his. "Six," she said starkly. "No, I lie—seven. I have lost Loyal, also."

Barta's mother, Essa, gasped, and a sound very like a sob came from her younger brother Talorc's throat.

A moment of horrified silence endured before Radoc spoke again, grief heavy in his voice. "Six? Name them!"

"My good friends: Dak, Munait, and Dort, as well as three others who agreed to come: Nectan, Gnith, and Gulb."

"Six of our best young warriors! Lost, you say? And your good hound."

Barta almost wished her father would rise up and strike her then. She could scarcely feel worse. Yet her eyes remained dry, the pain in her heart bursting. She could scarcely think about Loyal, left behind. But she had to get past this terrible confession, persuade her father to send men to fetch him.

Her father no doubt understood her grief even if his feelings could not touch what she felt. Radoc had always raised hounds and valued them highly. Even now his favorite, Bright, lay at his side and within reach of his hand. Aged, Bright had a white muzzle and like her master no longer went to battle.

Bright it had been who whelped the litter that included Loyal.

Barta fancied the bitch's eyes regarded her with as much accusation as her father's. Did the hound comprehend her son would never return?

Never.

Barta swayed on her feet and nearly fell. Only determination kept her upright.

Her mother, Essa, spoke for the first time since Barta had entered the dwelling. "Enough." Essa turned to face her husband. "Your daughter is wounded. You may continue to berate her later."

Radoc focused his hard gaze on Essa, and Barta

11

felt their clash of wills. Caledonii women had a fair say in the welfare of their tribes, and Barta's mother possessed a wise heart. Not often did Radoc disregard her advice. Just as rarely did she back down. Yet her life hadn't been easy since Radoc lost the use of his legs.

The ongoing war with the western Gaels had made life easy for none of them.

Essa laid a hand on Barta's shoulder; Barta swayed again.

Radoc blustered, "She deserves to carry her wounds as punishment. She needs to learn the consequences of her heedlessness. No girl—no matter how well she may fight—takes it into her head to launch a raid, especially behind the backs of her brother and me."

Barta wetted her lips. "I thought we could catch their scouting party unawares when they ventured over the border." Unofficial border that was—held merely by skirmishes just like this one.

Radoc's dark eyes blazed. "And what think you now of that decision?"

"Bad. It was a bad choice. But I thought—" Frustrated with the caution of her father and older brother, Wick, she'd thought she could demonstrate her worth as well as show the Gaels the folly of intruding any further onto Epidii territory. They'd already come far enough.

She glanced at Wick, silent all this while. Though their father still held the reins of leadership, Wick had in truth become their war chief. He and Barta enjoyed an easy, close relationship, but she'd gone behind his back in this. Did he look angry? Hard to tell.

He'd flinched when she spoke the names of the men lost—all his friends as well as hers. Now his face remained expressionless.

"I am sorry," she said as much to Wick as her father. "If I could do it over again—"

"What is done is done," Essa said heavily. "All that is left is the grieving. And there will be grieving."

"I know." Barta dropped her head. One of the men lost had been set to wed come winter; another had just fathered a son.

And she—she had lost Loyal.

Radoc spoke again. "It is no honor, daughter, to be the only warrior returned home from a battle. Why did you not die with your fellows?"

Barta jerked her chin back up. "Loyal saved me. He sacrificed himself, laid his body over mine. The Gaels thought me dead. Father," she leaned toward him urgently, "we must mount a rescue."

"Rescue?"

"A retrieval. We have to go back and fetch their bodies so we may afford them the honor they deserve."

"You skulk away with your life and dare speak to me of honor? You make me sick."

Barta's younger brother, Talorc, gave his father a stare. Tally and Barta were also close, yet even he did not venture a word in her defense.

"But Father," Barta argued, urged by her heart, "we must bring them home before—before the crows come or before the Gaels return to fetch the rest of their dead. For they had dead as well, I do assure you. We did sting them."

"Sting? Seven valiant lives lost for a sting?" Radoc barked at his wife, "Get her out of my sight."

"Come, Daughter."

Essa's fingers tightened on Barta's shoulder and coaxed her toward the deeper part of the hut. Aching, Barta stumbled away.

Essa pushed her down on a rug and lit a rush light. "Show me your wounds."

"I care nothing for my—"

"So I dare say, but they must be tended."

"Loyal..."

Suddenly the truth of it hit her; the big hound always at her side would never stand there again. Worse, she'd been forced to leave him cold and alone, could not even bring him home.

That knowledge shattered the numbness that had kept her upright before her father and choked her with tears. She cast herself down and gave way to the wracking grief—all she could expect to know from this day forward.

****

In the darkness where he floated, Loyal heard his mistress weeping. The darkness wasn't complete; it contained points of light scattered here and there that moved toward and past him, making him feel as if he alone stood still.

Not a good sensation. He'd always delighted in movement, in running and leaping, the sheer joy of feeling his muscles respond. He enjoyed his strength and vitality. That loss hurt almost as much as the separation from Barta.

Though they weren't completely separated. He could still hear her at a terrible distance. He wanted his muzzle right against her knee, his head beneath her hand.

He possessed no muzzle, no body now. Unsatisfactory. He needed to follow Barta, follow back the silver cord of magic he still saw stretching between them—unbroken.

He needed to rise.

Please. He addressed the magic that surrounded him, and the air brightened. The points of light slowed and gathered. Beneath him the darkness began to clear.

He looked down and saw—

The battlefield where he and his mistress had just been. All the objects there glittered in the shine from a sharp moon—metal work on the wrecked chariots, cast off and broken weapons.

A growl tried to stir within him and found no means for expression. He hated the chariots that inflicted so much harm and pain. Why could he not growl?

Looking again, he saw why, saw the body of a great, brindle hound sprawled on the ground, throat gaping, all the blood drained away. That must be him.

Never to leap and run again. Never to follow his mistress.

He howled at that, a wail of pain and protest, a spiritual rather than physical cry. The physical, it seemed, had ended for him. The pain had not.

Ahead of him, the light continued to gather. The glimmering sparks coalesced into a hazy form.

At first he thought it his mistress, for it felt—and looked—female. But though he'd always seen an aura around Barta, and had become attuned to it, she never shone so bright.

Beautiful. That thought arced through him, closely followed by *magical.* He knew perfectly well magic did exist, could not imagine why people sometimes doubted it. How did they suppose their world functioned without magic?

The woman who took form had long, flowing hair the color of the moonlight and skin that shone with the moon's radiance. She, he understood, was the moon taken tangibility.

The goddess.

He bowed to her as he must. Barta had always followed this goddess faithfully, praying to her when they walked together at night and whispering entreaties before every battle. That he understood. A hound obtained what he believed he would obtain, including favor. Barta's goddess was his also.

Now the goddess called to him, just as Barta always had. This call, though, he could answer.

Suddenly he stood before the woman made of moonlight. She wore nothing save the shawl of her hair. Her eyes contained wisdom and compassion.

Loyal.

The speaking of his name sounded through him like a chime of music. He liked music. It made his mistress happy, changed her scent, and altered the color of her aura.

Here, lady. He spoke without words, as he often did to Barta. Like Barta, the lady understood.

Why do you cry to me?

Did you hear me, lady?

I did, all the way up in my lofty perch where I sat mending my gown so I might dance again. You grieve.

I have lost her, lady. And she, me. I cannot endure it.

And she? Can she bear your parting?

Nay. He knew that above all things. He could taste Barta's pain.

She caused your death.

I do not believe that. And I do not care. I existed for her. I do, yet.

You no longer exist, faithful one. Make up your mind to it. Your spirit will move on. Best to prepare for that.

I cannot move on. I exist for her alone, he insisted.

The lady pondered that with pursed lips. Consideration pooled in her eyes.

Look, see, he pointed out, *the cord still stretches between us.*

It will fade, given time.

No.

You have been a good and faithful hound, as I say. I will grant you one boon. You may be allowed to come back and watch her from time to time.

He thought about that: more ache than boon. To see Barta and not be able to touch her was not enough and would not satisfy him.

I want to follow the cord before it fades.

You cannot. You have no body.

Grant me one.

The lady trembled in the air like a beam of moonlight when someone walks through it.

I did not hear you aright, hound. I thought you made a demand of me.

Not a demand, lady. A request. You say I have earned a boon.

You have.

Let me go back to her—in another body, if my old one be spoiled. I do not care what form. Only let me be with her, stand by her, continue to defend her against all peril.

The lady smiled. *You blame her not for your death?*

I blame her for nothing, ever.

That is because you were a hound. It would be different, were you a person with a complicated heart and mind. The lady appeared to ponder. *An interesting premise.*

Lady please, I implore you—before it is too late. Let me return to her.

Do you suppose I have the power to grant such a desire?

I believe you have the power to achieve anything.

Ah, Loyal—your unwavering belief has always been your greatest strength. It does deserve a reward.

Then send me back to her, I beg.

The lady debated it. He saw her glitter like light on water, and he prayed. All the while the silver cord stretched tighter but did not break.

Very well, said the lady at last. *But there must be conditions...*

Chapter Three

"You have to come with me, Gant, please. Now, before it is too late. We have to collect his body—their bodies—before the Gaels return. We owe them that, at the very least."

Gant balked where he sat in the long, half-subterranean hall—the place where Barta and her friends frequently gathered. Dak, Munait, and Dort, who lay in their blood, back with Loyal, usually also passed the time here with them as did less often those others now dead.

Never to do so again—and all Barta's fault. It had been in this very room she'd talked the young warriors into the raid that had ended so disastrously. Here she'd convinced them to keep it from her brother Wick, as well—he who would have been bound to take it to his father's ears.

At the beginning she'd tried to persuade them all, including these others now gathered. Wick, and Brude—one of the most senior among them—had slapped the idea down. But once most of the cooler heads, with her best friend Gant, left for their beds or to take up stints at guard duty, she'd told those three so close—so dear—to her it was their chance to act rather than sit back taking orders, to show the invaders their tribe would not run. Together, they'd convinced Nectan, Gnith, and Gulb, out in the dark.

Did the young men she now faced blame her for the loss of their friends? Undoubtedly. Did they despise her? She could not tell.

Neither did she care. Desperation filled her, so fierce it stung her eyes.

She would not weep here before these men. Only Gant had seen her weep in the past—best of friends from the age of four, he'd observed all her various hurts and frustrations.

She gazed into his eyes, searching for a spark of hope. He had a plain face liberally marked with tattoos, a scruffy, dark-red beard, and a nose once broken—her fault also—when a leather ball flew awry. Unlovely but precious to her was Gant. For the past two years, everyone in the tribe had expected them to wed. But the relationship, though close, wasn't that kind.

She said to him alone, "We must go now. Before long the sun will be up and the crows will come. Even before the enemy it will be the crows—I do not want him desecrated."

"Him?" Brude, who considered himself best among these young Epidii warriors, spoke in the sharp, quick way he had and lifted one brow. Barta would have preferred to do her begging without him present, but needs must. "You speak of your hound even ahead of our friends. Do they not also concern you, who defied all our advice and lured them to their deaths?"

"To be sure." Barta flushed with mortification and reminded herself her feelings weren't important. "I wish to retrieve all of them and bring them home with honor."

"You say you fear the Gaels will return to fetch their dead?" asked Urgast sharply. "Why did they not take them in the first place, if they were victorious?"

Barta drew herself up. "I did not say they were victorious."

"Yet," Brude took it up swiftly, "all of our party were slain—excepting you, of course."

"And many of theirs also—some lie still on the ground. I imagine when they withdrew they fetched away as many as they could. Their party was far larger than we expected, else I do not doubt we would have bested them. But we wrecked most of their chariots."

"I am sorry about Loyal," Gant said in his soft rumble. "It is a terrible loss."

"And a heavy price to pay for your rashness and lack of wisdom," Brude interrupted. "Did I not warn you a raid was folly?" He gestured at himself and the others. "Is that not why we refused to go with you—all but those hotheads who now lie dead? They have paid for their loyalty. And all because you wanted to snatch some glory."

Barta staggered back a step precisely as if Brude had struck her. "It was not about glory but about stinging the enemy. Showing them we are not afraid. And you can say nothing to chastise me more sharply than I chastise myself."

"Mayhap not." Brude shot Barta a measured glance. "So now accept the consequences, as must we—the loss of six brave men and your good hound." He sneered. "A woman does not belong on the battlefield—not even the daughter of a chief."

"Now," said Gede, the biggest of them and the last to speak, "has she not always fought valiantly at our sides?" He gave Barta a sympathetic look. "She and Loyal."

"Our women," Barta told Brude stiffly, "have never been loath to take a stand beside their men, be it armed with iron or magic."

"You'd be wiser keeping to magic," Brude replied.

"So you say," Barta replied with hard dignity. "But I do better with iron in my hand."

Brude snorted. "No fit recommendation. If you are so courageous, why were you the only member of our party to survive?"

Barta swallowed convulsively. "Knocked senseless; Loyal lay over me, and the enemy must have thought me dead."

"She bears many wounds." Tally, who must have followed Barta here and had no doubt been listening at the door all the while, entered the hut behind her. "I watched my mother tend them. You have no notion how hard my sister battled, Brude."

"Yet, whelp, she managed to save herself."

"Loyal saved her. Do you doubt his courage also?"

Brude smiled tightly. "No one here could ever question that. But your sister must learn the price of her thoughtlessness. It seems the goddess has drawn for her a sharp lesson."

Tally stiffened in every limb. "Were she a woman to sit at her weaving, Master Brude, you would then mock her for her lack of strength."

Gede rumbled to life. "There is something, Brude, in what the boy says."

Tally turned to Barta. "I will accompany you, sister, to retrieve our dead. I am not afraid."

"Neither do you have any more wisdom than your sister," put in Urgast. "It is far too risky, boy."

Barta turned to him. "I cannot leave Loyal's body

there. But no, Tally—neither will I let you endanger yourself."

Urgast grimaced. "She will not endanger her brother, nay, but has no such reservations about the rest of us."

The despair that gripped Barta's heart tightened in a stranglehold. "Very well, then, sit here like old men. I will retrieve Loyal on my own."

"And how carry him?" Urgast demanded.

"I shall construct a litter."

Gant hauled himself to his feet. "You will not go alone, Barta."

"Oh, by the goddess, Gant, thank you."

"And I," Tally insisted.

Gede, who made two of the lad in height and muscle, arose also. "I will come, but only if you stay here, boy." He ruffled Tally's hair.

"Oh, thank you, Gede." Barta turned to the big man. We'd best go at once, before we lose the cover of darkness." She eyed the others. "And if you will not come with us, please hold your tongues, at least—I beg you, not a word of this to my father or brother."

****

Barta smelled the battlefield even before she caught sight of it in the gloom. The reek of death hung over the place like a fog and froze the three of them in their tracks.

Gant put out a hand and clutched Barta's wrist. Into her ear he breathed, "Silently, now. We will move ahead and watch before we move closer."

She nodded. Blundering into a Gaelic party would mean capture or death.

But agonized frustration filled her to bursting. She

23

wanted to dash forward, gather their fallen, and be off away with them.

Instead they stood many long moments watching and—more importantly—listening. The sickle of moon had now set, and a faint glow edged the eastern horizon. Barta counted her heartbeats and prayed to the goddess: *Only let me hold him again, alive or dead.*

At last Gant nudged her. "Lead us to them. Softly."

She moved forward without sound through a scene even more terrible than she remembered—staring eyes and rent flesh, all in black and gray.

They came first upon Dak, a shattered spear still in his hand. Gede tugged him off by the shoulders, with Dak's heels dragging on the ground. Munait and Dort had fallen close together, as they had lived. Gant touched each gently on the head and hissed, "Where is Loyal?"

"Just here. We were all…" Barta stopped speaking abruptly. The four of them—and herself—had fallen nearly within arm's reach of one another, making a last stand. The hound's great body should be stretched just here.

It was not.

She spun on her heels, disoriented. No shaggy, brindle form lay anywhere within sight.

"He was here."

"Not here now." She felt rather than heard Gant's words, barely above a breath. "Are you certain—?"

"Yes. I crawled out from under him. Dort and Munait were beside me when I got to my feet."

"Then—"

"What, Gant, what?" Barta's heart leaped sickeningly. "Was he alive after all? Did he arise and follow after me?" But she had seen that terrible wound at his throat and knew he was dead.

Gant shook his head. "Maybe the Gaels came back and took him."

"That cannot be. You can see they have not yet been back to collect the rest of their own dead."

Gede loomed beside them. "What is it?"

"Loyal's body is gone."

"Impossible. No one's been here ahead of us."

"He was just here…"

"You must be mistaken."

Barta caught a glimpse of the tattoo on Gede's cheek as he stooped and gathered Munait into his arms. His muscles bulged.

"I am not mistaken." Tears flooded Barta's eyes. "Gant—"

"Hush, now. He must be still alive."

"No. No, he had nearly bled dry."

"We must get away," Gede grunted.

"But I cannot leave!"

"Whatever the mystery, Loyal is not here now. Help me, Gant."

The two men hauled their fallen comrades, one by one, away from the place of death to the cart they had brought, Gede pulling it like a pony. Barta stood as if rooted until Gant returned and tugged her arm, hard.

"Do you wish to get us all killed?"

That was the last thing she wanted. She bore, already, burdens enough.

Chapter Four

"What are we to do with her?" Barta caught the words her mother whispered to her father, even though Essa did not intend her to overhear.

Night had come once again to the settlement. Three days—and three endless nights—had now passed since the ill-advised raid in which Loyal had been lost. The six slain young warriors had been honored and buried, Barta forced to witness the grief that descended on those who loved them—and to bear the blame. Loyal's absence haunted her and deepened her despair, a relentless echo of pain.

Radoc's only response came in a grunt. Nights, as Barta knew, proved difficult for him when pain wracked his ruined body. Their tribe had been engaged in the struggle for land against the westerners most of Barta's life. At this moment, Radoc did not seem inclined to spare attention for his daughter's plight.

Essa went on, no doubt supposing Barta, who lay in her sleeping alcove, in fact slept.

"She refuses to get out of bed; she will take nothing to eat. She will not speak," Essa fretted.

"She is grieving and bearing a heavy share of guilt. Is that so hard to understand? We all grieve in our own ways, and it was a heavy loss for her, this one." Barta knew, without looking, that her father reached out his hand to caress the head of his bitch, Bright, never far from his side. Radoc's other dog, Strength, who had perished in the same battle that saw Radoc crippled, had been given a funeral with great ceremony. Something Barta would not be able to do for Loyal.

Her stomach clenched and soured as it did every time she thought of her failure to bring Loyal home, or pictured the empty place on the field where his great form should have been lying. Questions began running through her head again: what had happened to him? Could he have been alive when she left him? Had he lived long enough to drag himself away into the dark and then perished? Should she go search again?

If the enemy had come and collected his body— then why? Why take the body of a slain hound and yet leave their own dead behind?

Barta thought their leader—the warrior with the fierce eyes and the flying yellow hair—had taken a significant injury near the end of the battle. Perhaps that explained why the Gaels had withdrawn so abruptly.

It didn't explain Loyal's missing corpse.

"Perhaps a new pup," her mother whispered. "Are any of your hounds due to whelp?"

Radoc grunted again. "She does not want a new pup—at least not yet. I tell you again, Essa, leave her be."

"But"—Essa's whisper became more urgent—"she shows no signs of coming out from her darkness."

"It has been three days. Would you not grieve that long for one you loved, Wife? Would you not grieve so for me?"

Barta knew, also without looking, her mother replied with a kiss even before her words. "I, husband, would be devastated beyond expressing."

"Well, then."

"But what if this affects her for good? Barta has always been so fierce and bold."

"And now she learns the price of such boldness. I tell you again, Wife, let—"

Radoc broke off in midsentence. Outside the dwelling a furor had arisen, splitting the quiet night—cries of challenge and alarm, exclamations that caught even Barta's bruised attention.

Radoc swore; Essa got to her feet, and Tally stirred. Barta's older brother, Wick, directed the night watch and so was absent from his bed.

"Help me up," Radoc told his wife.

Barta, not thinking of herself for the first time in days, went to assist her mother. No easy task, getting Radoc up from his pallet once he had retired for the night. Both women struggled, and Tally hurried to help also, his dark eyes wide with alarm.

"What is happening, Father?" he asked. "Are we under attack?"

"Don't know. Get your weapons."

They all went outside into a scene Barta could not immediately comprehend. The waxing moon sailed overhead in a clear night sky, its silver light filtering down between the branches of the trees beneath which the huts sheltered. It pricked out a troop of Epidii guards hauling in a captive.

A stranger.

Barta froze where she stood, one shoulder lodged beneath her father's arm, and stared. The most peculiar sensation swept over her. A stranger, yes—and yet not.

"What goes on here?" Radoc bellowed.

Wick, who held the strange man fast by one arm,

replied, "We caught him approaching the settlement, bold as you please. Says he has come to offer his service."

"Is that so?"

By now the entire settlement—some two and a half score strong, from infants to elders—had emerged from their huts. All stared.

The stranger stood tall, topping even Wick's impressive height, and strongly made though without bulk. His hair, a shaggy mane, looked almost silver in the mystical light, and he seemed unaffected by the furor he occasioned. Obviously of Caledonii blood, he wore a number of weapons along with tattoos that must denote his tribe.

Nothing else.

Barta caught her breath. She'd seen her share of naked men—her brothers and also others among the warriors, during wrestling contests or at play. Never any male who matched this.

A messenger, perhaps? But why should he come to them unclothed and in the middle of the night?

"He says nothing more," Wick reiterated. "Only that he offers his service."

"Who are you?" Radoc addressed the stranger directly. "Why have you come?"

The stranger tipped his head slightly as if gauging the emotions in Radoc's voice. He had a handsome, narrow face, deeply set eyes, and brows that slanted upward. He also possessed graceful hands that dangled at his sides but made no move to reach for his weapons—a long knife and, strapped at his ankle, what the westerners called a dirk.

Even his feet, long and slender, were bare.

He made no reply to Radoc's query.

"Do you come from one of the northern tribes?" Radoc pressed. "What is the name of your chief?"

The stranger stepped forward out of Wick's grasp. He placed one hand over his heart, where lay a bold tattoo, bright even in the moonlight, as if it alone should identify him.

"I come, Chief Radoc, to take the place of another who has been lost."

Without further words, the beautiful young man knelt at Barta's feet.

****

All the agony that had filled him since his death as a hound now eased for the first time. Finding himself once more where he was meant to be, he felt as if he could breathe again and everything became right—save for his bewilderment. Why did his mistress fail to recognize him?

Out of all the confusion and the new sensations assaulting him, this stood out. To be sure, the Lady had warned him the journey he undertook would prove challenging. He must learn to use language, walk upright, and deal with human nuances. She'd said Barta would not know him and that he could not tell her who he was.

He hadn't believed it, though. Barta couldn't fail to know him in any form—human or otherwise. He'd believed in that so fiercely he'd even extracted a promise from the Lady that should Barta guess his identity, he could then tell her how he had gained this chance to return to her.

Return to her.

That, indeed, had been all that mattered to him—

the pull of the silver cord that still connected them, an irresistible summons quite clearly reaching past death.

But now he knelt at her feet—a place he'd crossed from the far country to reach—and she stared at him as at a stranger.

She will know me, he'd vowed to the goddess, *as soon as she looks into my eyes.*

So far, Barta had looked anywhere but. She'd gazed at the ground or at his body which to him seemed both magnificent and terribly limiting. She'd looked at his hair—everywhere but into his eyes, even though he compelled her with his gaze.

Skilled as he was at reading signs, he could sense her great discomfort and her sorrow. Why? Was he not still him? And had he not returned to her?

For a time. At great cost.

He would not think about that now. Thought proved far too difficult, given all those odd impulses and implications pressing at him. In the past his thoughts had possessed no implications. Black and white were just that—black and white.

"Get up," Master Radoc bellowed at him.

Used from birth to obeying, he nevertheless remained where he was, his gaze fixed on Barta.

"Get up," she whispered fiercely, "for the sake of the goddess."

For Her sake, and hers.

He rose to his feet and stood waiting for instructions. Barta still had not met his gaze.

"What is your name?" Radoc growled.

He thought about that. Forbidden to give his former name, he had no other.

He smiled at Barta. "I do not know. I am here at

my mistress's service; let her name me."

Barta's eyes widened, and she recoiled. Had that been the wrong thing for him to say?

"From what tribe do you hail?" Radoc demanded, even as those gathered around them muttered.

Better prepared for this, he spoke the name the Lady had given him. "Bilii."

"From north of the Pitcairn?" Radoc's eyes narrowed. "Who sent you?"

"I was called by my Mistress Barta's need."

That caused more muttering. He heard the word "magic" pass many lips.

Magic they should comprehend; it existed everywhere in the world, in the sound of the wind passing over the land, in the flight of a bird, in the rhythm of his own heartbeat. He stood now doubly bound by it.

But bound mostly by love. He continued to gaze at his mistress, willing her to see that.

He'd existed for her all his life and never found her stupid. Indeed, usually her wits moved most swiftly and matched his in daring. Now she either could not or would not understand.

"It is some trick," whispered Brude. "He has been sent by the enemy to penetrate our defenses." He drew his short knife. "I say kill him at once."

And was this a threat? Not to his mistress but to him directly—which threatened her in turn. He spun to face Brude and growled.

"Yet," said Tally, "if he bears the marks of a tribe we know, how can he then be an enemy?"

Brude snorted. "Foolish boy—that is part of the trickery. Leave him alone with Barta, and he will slit her throat at his first chance."

Mistress Essa pressed forward to stand in front of him. She peered into his eyes even as Barta refused to do, and caught her breath. "Oh, by the goddess…"

Relief filled him again; Mistress Essa understood enchantment and possessed a great deal of wisdom. Surely she could glean his identity.

"What is it, Ma?" Barta asked, fearfully.

Essa snagged Barta's hand.

"Bring him into our hut, Husband. We will find him some clothing and offer him a place at our hearth."

Chapter Five

"You must have a name, everyone does. Why would you ask me to give you another one?"

The stranger stared at Barta in that compelling way he had, the gaze she found it so difficult to avoid. The two of them sat beside her parents' hearth, alone for the moment—alone for the first time.

Tally had fallen asleep before Wick carried him off to his sleeping bench and remained there as if on guard over the boy. Her parents, in their own alcove, spoke intently in tones too low for Barta to understand.

The beautiful young man sat within arm's reach of Barta. Oh, and he was beautiful despite the fact that Essa had lent him some of Radoc's old clothing.

He had wild hair of ashen brown, cropped unevenly and looking rough to the touch, though Barta just knew if she buried her fingers there it would prove soft and beguiling. A foreign slant lay in the elegant sculpting of his narrow face, but it was strangely familiar for all that. He moved with inexplicable grace, his long limbs, even covered with clothing, like music in motion.

His eyes...

But after the merest flicker of a glance, Barta could not look there, even though he continued that most intent stare. Whatever lay in his eyes, she felt unready to encounter it.

Magic, as the others said or something else darker, more sinister?

Yet the emotions she felt coming from him contained more reassurance than threat. That seemed familiar too, almost comforting. How could it be?

"Did something happen that caused you to forget your name?"

"Something most profound happened to me." His voice had a low pitch and a gravely sound that sent a delicate shiver up Barta's spine. He went on, "A battle. It affected my mind. I was sent here into your service to take the place of another."

Loyal. The name appeared unbidden in Barta's head. Well, it had not been far from her mind ever since she'd left him sprawled on the ground. To be sure, she had prayed for his return. But she wanted him, not some human substitution.

"Still, I do not think it my place to name you."

"But I am born anew here with you, my lady, and will be forever true to you." He hesitated. "Why will you not look at me?"

"I have. I will." She turned her face to him, her gaze slipping from his hair to his lips to the skin visible at the open neck of his tunic. "Can you not tell me, at least, who sent you?"

"I cannot."

"What do you remember of your past life?"

"I was a warrior and fought fiercely. I will do the same on your behalf."

Barta did not doubt that. Everything about him argued he would make a potent weapon in a battle.

"Here we are engaged in a desperate struggle to hold our land. The Gaels moving east from Dal Riada want this territory—they are greedy for it. So it is in the north also, I believe."

"Yes."

"This particular struggle has been going on most of my life, and yours, yes?"

He nodded. Slowly, as if struggling to remember, he said, "I cannot recall a time when there were not battles. The purpose of my life has been to fight, to defend."

"And whoever sent you—your tribeschief? How did he know we were in need of warriors?"

"Magic." The word came from behind Barta, uttered by her mother. Essa had come from her sleeping alcove and now stood regarding the two of them, her hair hanging loose down her back.

Standing so, she didn't appear old enough to have grown children. Indeed, at that moment Barta could not help but wonder how Essa must appear to the stranger, with her thick mane of russet hair and wide, gray eyes. Did she look like Barta's sister rather than her mother?

Essa sat down beside them and folded her hands gracefully. "Daughter, do not search for explanations that do not exist."

Barta stole another uneasy look at their guest before she said, "But his appearance here might be suspect, as Father says."

"Somehow I do not think so." Essa switched her gaze to the visitor. "If you are to remain with us, and near my daughter, you must prove yourself. Are you willing to do that?"

He inclined his head; the rough hair fell forward across his shoulders. "I am, Lady."

"If I set a trial, will you undergo it?"

"I will, Lady—anything you ask."

Barta spoke softly. "What kind of trial? Ma, what would you ask of him?"

Essa did not speak at once. "That," she said at last, "is just what your father and I have been discussing."

"But you are the one who said he's been sent by magic."

Essa smiled. "I need no convincing, Daughter. Others of the tribe will. We have only his word as to how or why he has been sent. And trust must be won, if he is to be accepted." Again she looked at the young man in question, meeting his gaze even as Barta avoided it. "I believe you do wish to stay?"

"Yes, Lady."

"But," Barta protested yet again, "to undergo a trial...it seems so hard." And why did she suddenly feel protective of the stranger? Certainly he appeared more than capable of looking after himself.

"Barta, many, like your father, suspect deception. I cannot say I blame them. Nor," she told their guest, "should you, young...man."

Again he bowed his head with almost regal grace. "I will undergo whatever trial you ask."

"Wait." Again protectiveness flared in Barta's heart. "Do not agree before you hear what you'll be asked to undertake. Ma?"

"That has yet to be determined. I must consult with those among us most likely to complain about his presence. Meanwhile, young man, I suggest you get what rest you can. I regret to say you must sleep outside until your loyalty is proven."

For the first time, protest touched the man's handsome features. An instant later he nodded yet again. "As you ask, Lady."

"But," Barta spoke despite herself, "it is cold outside."

"And he has journeyed far," Essa agreed. "Yet your father has asked the question, should we all lie down so he might slit our throats in our sleep? Would you, Barta, like to go and argue it with him?"

Barta shook her head. Why should it bother her so, the thought of the stranger lying in the cold? She did not know him. How could she care what happened to him?

The young man got to his feet. He spoke to Barta rather than to her mother. "It is all right. I do not mind."

"Wait." Barta hurried to her own sleeping bench, where she gathered up one of her rugs. She returned and pressed it into his hands. "To help ward off the cold."

He smiled, and it lit his face with wild beauty. He lifted the rug, pressed it to his face as if testing its warmth, and inhaled deeply. "Thank you. This will be a comfort."

Barta stood where she was as her mother led him to the door. Why should it hurt physically to watch him go? He would not be far away; she would see him come morning.

With that sustaining thought lodged in her head she went to her sleeping bench. Morning could not come soon enough.

****

The moon had narrowed to a sharp crescent, a mere fingernail hanging low in the sky. From where he lay he could just see it through the trees that screened the Epidii settlement. Mostly hazel they were, and possessed of potent magic.

Before his transformation at the Lady's will, he'd been able to sense magic clearly, just as he could smell the passing of a badger or hare. Now that ability had faded, yet it seemed he kept the awareness of where magic existed, gathered like a cloak around Essa and trailing everywhere throughout the camp. These folk lived by whispering prayers whenever they undertook any action. They wove spells of protection as easily as they breathed. He used to be able to see the magic clearly. Though he no longer could, its shadows gathered before his eyes.

In the past he had not prayed, at least not consciously. He'd merely spoken to the Lady when he felt the need.

As when Barta had left him lying on the bloodied ground.

Did he need to begin praying now? Must he mutter words and cast spells using this strange new medium of language that he found so difficult? Could he no longer speak to the Lady, or to Barta, with his mind?

No matter—it did not make too great a price to pay, if he could be near Barta. Nothing would make too high a price. Even if he must lie here outside the door, separated from her by wattle and leather, he could feel her nearness. And her scent lay in the rug she'd given him from her own bed.

He buried his face in it again and inhaled. How many times had he lain with her in that bed? Only from puppyhood. He remembered how she'd laughed when he grew yet still strove to push his great limbs in with her, leaving her less and less space.

Contentment lay in that memory. And longing. But

she was just inside—he could endure this night.

He wondered what Lady Essa would propose as a trial for him. He suspected he should pray about that. But he merely lay with his eyes on the sliver of moon and breathed Barta's scent.

He wished she'd given him a name. For he could no longer use the one by which she had first called him.

Chapter Six

Rain began to fall before morning, clouds preceding the dawn and obscuring the new sun. He awoke from a brief, fitful sleep, drenched to the skin and with a row of children staring at him, their shaggy heads in a line.

He knew them all, though of course they did not recognize him. He, along with his canine brothers and sisters, had played with them in the past, frolicked and chased. Now he dared not let on.

They looked far too solemn and wary, and behind them, keeping a careful eye, stood their fathers and elder brothers.

He roused himself, trying to gather his wits and control these strange new senses—the severely limited ability to capture scent, the overload of touch.

He sat up, and one of the children said to another, "He sleeps across the doorway like a hound."

So he did.

He risked a smile at the children, and they scattered like mist, wild as puppies. Their elders, farther back, lingered. What did they expect he might do? Fly at his hosts and slit their throats?

Consulting this odd new body of his, he found conflicting impulses. The Lady had healed his battle wounds when she transformed him; he felt only residual pain. But hunger competed fiercely with the need to piss. Which call should he satisfy first?

He did not suppose it would be acceptable to lift his leg on the nearest tree as he had in the past. If he made a dash for the surrounding forest, he suspected he might come under attack.

He got to his feet, testing that supposition, and the watching Epidii tensed.

Just then, a hound came strolling by, one of those belonging to Gede, who was friend to Wick. The dog, named Mighty, checked and looked at him, hackles rising. Pure, baffled consternation shone from Mighty's eyes, and a growl of puzzlement issued from his jaws.

The door of the dwelling opened abruptly; Barta peered out, and relief flooded him.

"Oh, you are awake," she whispered. "Mother said to let you in."

He gestured to himself. "Thank you, but first I need—"

"Yes, very well. I will show you the midden."

To be sure, he knew where that lay. He wrinkled his nose involuntarily at the prospect of going near that stinking place. But he would follow her anywhere and did so now, as if commanded.

How strange it felt to be moving at her side as he always had, to adjust his stride to match hers once again, yet to be taller than she!

He measured every movement of her arms and legs—slender, strong, and long for those of a female person—and concentrated on catching her delectable scent. That became more difficult when they neared the pit near the edge of the trees, where folk came to relieve themselves and the night pots got emptied.

Still, the place did not smell as bad as he

remembered. Could there be advantages to this new, stunted form he occupied?

Barta turned her back, while he did as he must, and waited to accompany him back again. The rain continued to fall, pelting down softly. When he returned to her side, he saw it caressed her cheeks like tears.

However hampered his senses might be, it seemed he had no trouble reading her emotions, which came to him as easily as ever. He could almost taste her grief and uncertainty.

At least she seemed more willing to look at him this morning. In fact, her gaze inspected his face as if she searched him for something, though her eyes still had trouble meeting his for more than an instant.

"Come along," she bade.

"Mistress, have you chosen for me a name?"

Her uncertainty flared, edged with distress. "I still do not see why I should. It does not seem appropriate."

"If I had a name, I have forgotten it." A lie. Loyal. He ached to hear it from her lips, but it seemed this new tongue of his lent itself to deception.

She gave him a rebellious look. Indeed, he knew his mistress for rebellious at the best of times. Now she said, "Perhaps you will recall the name you had."

He slowed his steps to a halt. She paused with him. Earnestly, he said, "Whatever name I may have had is mine no more. For me, that life is done. I begin anew here, with you. And I promise you, I will prove true to you every day we spend together."

Light flared in her eyes for an instant, obscuring her sorrow. "Is it so?" She tossed her head, recapturing some of the spirit he loved to see. "Then perhaps I should call you 'True' and be done."

He stared at her compellingly. The name "True" would please him very well. "I will go by that name, and happily."

But she concluded, "And what kind of name is that for a man? Let us see how you prove yourself in this trial my mother has in mind before I go naming you, eh?"

He only stared at her. True he was, from that moment.

They entered Radoc's dwelling—Barta first, with him on her heels—and the familiar scents of the place assailed him, though not as strongly as they used to. Mistress Essa had a meal prepared; she looked up at them sharply.

"There you are. I'd begun to wonder if our new arrival had flown."

"I needed to show him around the encampment."

"Of course. Sit down, young man. You are welcome to share our breakfast."

Was he welcome, though? He felt a measure of that emotion flowing from Essa and in a lesser amount from Tally. The others stared at him with suspicion.

Chief Radoc, as he very well knew suffered greatly from his afflictions upon rising. He groaned now as he struggled to shift his bulk and glared at everyone impartially. But his glare at the newcomer seemed fiercest. Bright, who lay at the side of Radoc's bed, came to greet him with a touch of her nose to his hand, her eyes matching her name. Ah, and at least his mother still knew him.

"Sit here beside me," Barta said softly and brushed his arm with her hand. His entire body leaped to attention. Used as he was to her touch, he'd never before experienced it skin on skin. His overloaded senses made him flush.

But they settled beside the hearth, and Tally took the place on his other side. Mistress Essa passed out food; True ate ravenously, shoving in the barley mash, using the strange appendages of his fingers.

He paused when he noticed the others eyeing him askance. He wondered if he broke some misunderstood rule of hospitality.

Mistress Essa spoke. "Forgive me, young man. We were remiss in failing to offer you a repast last evening. You journeyed far and were clearly famished."

He gazed at her. "I am content, Mistress, with whatever you are willing to offer me."

"Starve him then," Wick muttered, not quite under his breath.

Essa filled a bowl for Radoc, who cleared his throat and eyed Wick.

"Your mother has persuaded me we owe our guest a full measure of hospitality—at least until he proves himself unworthy."

"That, Master, I will never do."

Radoc fixed him with a fierce eye, offering a glimpse of the spirit that survived his dire injuries. "We shall see. Are you prepared to accept today's challenge?"

"How can he be prepared?" asked Tally. "He knows not what you will ask of him."

"I am prepared—no matter what it may be."

He felt more than saw Barta look at him. All at once he longed for her touch once again, reinforcing their sense of connection.

Tally handed over his breakfast. "Here—you need

this more than I do."

"I would not deprive you, young Master."

Tally gave him a crooked smile. "If I know my mother, you will need all your strength. And I would rather skip my breakfast and see you succeed."

Essa exclaimed in disapproval. "Keep your breakfast, son. Are we so poor we cannot provide our guest all he asks?"

Content, Tally settled back to eat even as Essa offered more food around the hearth.

True ate his second portion as ravenously as the first, wondering why Barta eyed him so strangely all the while. The drink offered—a strange, bitter brew—tasted vile, and he had difficulty sipping it from the rim of the cup as the others did. He wished he had water instead.

When finished, Radoc emitted a great belch and said, "There now. You had better tell the young man what you have in mind for him, my love, so he may better prepare himself."

Essa got to her feet. Barta arose also, and True stumbled up at her side, gaze fixed on Essa.

He had always seen so much in Mistress Essa's eyes which, like Barta's and Tally's, were a dark, smoky gray.

Now they glowed with wisdom. "We"—she gestured at herself and Radoc—"have decided to place your proving in the hands of the gods. You will undergo a threefold trial. If you pass all three parts, we will accept you into the tribe as one of our own. Should you fail any part, we will have to ask you to leave. Do you understand?"

Dismay flooded him. He did not want to risk

leaving Barta for any reason. But surely the goddess, having transformed him, would not allow him to fail?

He nodded.

Barta spoke swiftly. "What are these trials just?"

"He will be asked to prove his endurance, his determination, and his valor. Young man, in what order would you face these challenges?"

He thought about it. Used to employing sheer instinct rather than reason, he found the process difficult. Impulse made him say, "As spoken, mistress."

"Wait." Barta reached out and once more touched his arm lightly. He stiffened as if brushed by flame. "Is that the best order? Endurance, taken first, may tire you for the other challenges."

"Yet valor," Tally put in, "if that's combat, might wound him for the others."

Barta looked at her mother. "Why must he face this ordeal at all?"

His heart bounded. Did his mistress champion him? Like him, could she feel their connection?

Radoc answered, "Would you have us trust him without proving, Daughter? Allow him to sit by our hearth, where he might hear our secrets, give him leave to perhaps attack us in the night?"

Wick added, "If you expect the rest of the tribe to trust him, Barta, he must be tested."

"I do not mind," he told Barta. "The goddess will uphold me." And he would suffer far more—anything—to remain near her.

She studied him slowly, her gaze moving from his hair and down his body, lingering on his lips and chest, still avoiding his eyes.

"May the goddess be with you then."

47

He bowed his head to her, even as he might to that entity. "I ask you only to grant me the name of 'True,' should I come through this trial victorious."

Still her gaze measured him. "That I will most surely do."

Chapter Seven

He stood at the center of a circle made up of Epidii tribesfolk, all alone. They had taken back his borrowed clothing, save for a twist of fabric around his loins. That didn't bother him; being comfortable since birth in his hide, he barely noticed.

His separation from Barta bothered him far more. At least he could still see her, just across from him at the edge of the circle, beside young Master Tally.

His weapons bothered him also. A warrior since a pup, he had entered countless battles at Barta's side—but he'd fought with claws and jaws, never with cold iron. He had seen the tribesfolk employ knife, spear, and even sword often enough, but until now he'd never attempted to battle with those weapons in his hands.

Never had hands, for all that. Now he would face combat, he felt almost certain, but not yet. Not before he survived the other two challenges.

It would not be easy. Yet neither had it been easy persuading the goddess to let him cross back from the shadowy plain to be with Barta. He would do anything to retain this place.

He—and the hushed crowd—watched as Master Wick and the warrior called Brude approached with objects in their arms. From the way they walked, he could see those objects must be heavy. He got a good look when they dropped the things at his feet.

Rocks, each perhaps half the size of a large hound's head, and woven vine sacks.

No one made a sound as the two warriors thrust the rocks into the sacks. He stole a look at Barta and saw that her teeth worried her bottom lip.

When all seemed readied, Master Radoc addressed him. "Take a stance, both arms extended straight out from your sides. The test is to see if you can hold the sacks up longer than our strongest warrior—Gede."

Ah, and he knew Master Gede well, though of course that young man did not recognize him now. Gede—half a head taller than his fellows and rife with muscle—stepped into the ring and took up a stance facing him.

Doubt rushed his heart. How could he hope to outlast such a strong person?

He stole another look at Barta and saw dismay in her eyes. He shut his own eyes for an instant.

Great Lady, uphold me.

And he nodded his head.

****

Cruel. No one should have to endure such cruelty.

The sun, now well up on a lovely morning, illuminated the scene all too clearly. The two young men stood facing each other with their arms outstretched, stiff as if made of iron. Both had been loaded with sacks of rocks, three on each arm.

Barta had groaned inwardly as each sack was loaded. She never imagined the two men could last so long.

Now they both sweated even though the sun had not yet grown warm. Barta sweated in sympathy, the moisture gathering to trickle down between her shoulder blades and breasts.

Gede wore a frown that wrinkled his brow and grew heavier as the moments crept by. True—for so he wished to be called—kept his expression blank and set, his eyes wide. But not long since he'd parted his lips and begun to pant. And Barta had caught the merest tremble in his limbs, first the outstretched arms and then, almost imperceptibly, his legs.

Barta directed another look at her father—had he come up with this punishing scheme?—who also appeared impassive except for a faint scowl.

What if she spoke up, called on him to end this? Would it spoil the participants' concentration? That would be the last thing she wanted to do.

Unhappily, she examined her heart. She had no real reason to care for the young man who stood before them so courageously. No reason. Yet emotion burned inside her, and honesty bade her acknowledge she would do anything to aid him.

Just then his arms quivered more violently— enough that several of the sacks suspended from them swayed, which must be agonizing. The onlookers murmured—a few hooted—and Gede fixed his gaze on his opponent as if willing him to fail.

Barta found herself willing just the opposite.

Stand. Endure.

True's gaze moved to her as if he caught the essence of her thought. Then he closed his eyes and reset himself, the muscles in his arms, shoulders and back bunching.

Gede's frown deepened. He too looked at Barta, his auburn hair strung across his eyes, wet with perspiration.

A small breeze came from the east, threaded its way through the crowd, and caressed both men where they stood.

Despite that welcome relief, it was now Gede who swayed where he stood. His great stumps of legs—which might make two of his opponent's—began to shake, and he reset them, straining hard.

Please, Barta said in her mind. True remained with his eyes squeezed tight shut, face pale and set in every line.

She sensed he could not hold out much longer.

Gede looked at Barta again—just a flick of a glance—his scowl now a prodigious thing. Abruptly his outstretched arms jerked, and he lowered them. The sacks of rocks fell with a series of thuds.

The crowd gasped, as did Barta. Wick, who had stationed himself near her and Tally, swore bitterly. True opened his eyes, lowered his sacks, and sank to his knees.

Barta, feeling someone should, cried out, "Victorious! The newcomer is victorious."

"Aye, Daughter. Yet that is but the first challenge." Radoc gestured Wick over to him and began speaking in his ear furiously.

Barta debated what she should do. True still knelt where he had fallen. Would it be too much a mark of favor on her part if she went to him?

Before she could decide, Gede stepped forward and helped his former opponent to his feet. He slapped True on the back in congratulation.

Barta bit her lip again and eyed preparations for the next challenge. Would they not first allow the competitors to rest? Offer them water? But no, for great slabs of rock were being hauled in by a number of men, lashed with bindings.

No, oh, no.

An ancient challenge was this, some said as old as the standing stones that dotted the land, and as unyielding. It had in the past sometimes been used to test ponies, when the tribes had them—or hounds. The practice had been stopped as considered too cruel.

But they would use it now to challenge her champion.

Hers?

Fundamentally honest, Barta consulted her heart and conceded yes—oh, yes.

She stepped forward to her father's side and butted into his conversation with Wick.

"Father, you cannot do this."

Radoc looked at her, his dark gaze fathomless. "Daughter, stay out of it."

"But it is unfair. To both of them. You must allow Gede and the challenger time to rest."

Radoc grinned mirthlessly. "Gede can rest all his likes. As for the challenger, he offered himself up to this."

"I don't understand. Gede…"

Wick told her, "In this part of the challenge, the tribe will be represented by still another of our warriors."

"Unfair! Who…"

"Daughter, be silent!" Radoc barked loudly enough for everyone to hear.

"When have I ever been silent in the face of injustice? You taught me better."

Essa stepped forward and seized Barta's hand.

"Hush now, girl." She drew Barta aside and gazed into her eyes steadily. "If you would have that young man accepted here, it must be so."

Barta vocalized what she already felt in her heart. "I have already accepted him."

"I know. As have I."

"Yes?" Barta searched her mother's eyes.

"Have faith. Trust."

"But it is hard to see him used so sorely."

"Trust," Essa said again. "There is magic at play here."

"Very well." But Barta glanced again at the man who once more stood alone at the center of the circle. He watched her steadily with clear, hazel eyes.

"Believe," Essa whispered and squeezed her hand. "Now hold your tongue. They are ready to begin."

****

He ached fiercely from the first trial, and yet he could see they had the second test ready to begin. Memories shifted in his mind, and he knew he'd seen this before, though not recently. He had certainly never participated.

He wished desperately he might have a few moments respite before it began. But no—for the tribesmen had it all laid out—two great boulders strung with lines which ended in loops. The crowd thinned to form an alley rather than a circle, two lines of them. And a new opponent stepped out.

A new opponent. One fresh, his muscles not already screaming. He knew this man—to be sure, he knew and remembered them all. This one, called Gartnait, had never been a warrior. Old enough, almost, to be a contemporary of Radoc's, he melded iron for the tribe and performed what building services were needed. Too slow to fight, he nevertheless possessed prodigious strength.

"This trial," Radoc called out, "will prove the trait of determination. Which man will give up in the face of the impossible? One possesses youth but has already been hard used. The other is fresh but possesses age. Let us lay it before the gods."

In your hands, Lady, he thought. He jerked in surprise at finding Gede beside him; the big man nudged him into place in front of one of the boulders and threaded the lines over his shoulders and across his chest, a hint of kindness in his eyes.

"It will be difficult." Gede swept him with a look. "Maybe, as he says, impossible."

"It cannot be impossible," True replied. "Not if I am to win leave to stay."

Gede nodded gravely. "Best of good fortune, then."

Gartnait had also been strapped into his harness. A job for stout ponies was this, and Gartnait had legs like those of a cob.

Radoc bellowed, "The contest is this. My son, Wick, has scratched a line across the path yonder."

Indeed, and it did not look too far.

"The first man to drag his load across the line wins this leg of the competition."

"All the way across, Chief?" clarified Gartnait. "The whole stone?" he eyed his opponent. "I have done this before."

"The stone must clear the line." Radoc raised his hand before slashing it downward. "And—go!"

Chapter Eight

True threw all his weight into the ropes that confined him. They went taut before they bit deep into the flesh of his shoulders and chest. The boulder behind him did not so much as quiver.

Gartnait, beside him, did the same, emitting a mighty roar. But he got no better result.

An impossible task, to be sure. But the Lady knew nothing of impossible. Had she not turned him from a dead hound to a living man and returned him to Barta? Now he must exert himself to keep the place.

He put his head down, set his shoulders, and dug with his legs. This time he grunted a groan as every muscle strained. Instinct told him once he got the dead weight moving, half the battle would be won.

Did the boulder wiggle behind him? He was not sure, but Gartnait snarled another roar and stepped forward also. His load slid the merest hair.

True could not let the strong man win, not if it lost him Barta's company. Despair possessed him for an instant and transformed into determination.

In the past he'd done anything and everything to be with her—broken out of a hut using his teeth, stumbled behind her dragging a wounded paw. Only once had he failed to follow her anywhere. He would make up for that now.

He felt his heart swell in his chest and threw

himself into the traces, all his love behind it. His load moved.

The onlookers exclaimed, and he heard Barta's voice among the others. The straps bit as he strained once more.

Gartnait, ahead of him by perhaps a step, dug harder, his stone grinding forward and dragging the earth with it.

The finish line which had looked so close now seemed an unreachable distance. So hard, so far. How could he do this?

Ah, but he must.

He dug his toes in more fiercely, tired muscles screaming. He thought of his former life, running over the hills at his mistress's side, every limb fresh and functioning at peak. He thought of the sheer joy of movement. He prayed.

Lady...please.

Strength flooded through him like a stream of magic, stopping the tremble in his legs, pumping his lungs full of air. He took another step, two steps, and came level with Gartnait.

He heard Master Gede bellow in approval. He thought of Barta and bunched his muscles again. He felt the traces tear the skin of his shoulders.

Pain.

Ignore it. You've ignored pain for her sake before. So it had been that time he took a sword stroke on his head, just above his ear—the blood had nearly blinded him. He'd kept fighting at her side. Scars, he had them. None mattered.

Another step, head tucked fiercely down—his toes touched the line. Still an impossible distance to drag the load the length of the ropes and the lashed stone itself. The pain in his shoulders flared like fire. He closed his mind to it and imagined himself running at Barta's side. He fixed on that image, blotting out everything else.

He saw Gartnait from the corner of his eye, staggering just behind him, and blotted that out also.

Another dragging step and another. A great roar filled his ears. His blood pounding, or the onlookers? Breath tore from his lungs, and his load ground to a halt.

Had he failed?

He opened eyes squeezed shut all this while—they stung with sweat—and saw Barta's face before him, wide-eyed.

"You did it. Oh, by the goddess, you did!"

He turned, shoulders ablaze, and looked behind at the load. The line scribed in the dirt had been rubbed out where the stone dragged across but could still be seen on either side. His stone had cleared it—Gartnait's had halted half way.

He sank to his knees.

Barta fell with him, her hand still on his shoulder. "Father, he must have a respite."

Radoc hollered something in reply; he could not hear what for the noise made by the onlookers. But he felt Barta stiffen.

"Impossible!" she yelled back. "I must have a chance to dress his wounds."

He did hear Radoc's reply. "Do so then, but swiftly."

Barta carefully eased the cruel straps from his shoulders, the skin there torn raw. Ignoring that, he gazed into her eyes. What did he see? Concern. A

58

measure of kindness. Anger on his behalf.

She cared about him. Suddenly his hurts mattered not at all. He had accomplished the first two tasks. He could do anything if he believed she wanted him at her side.

A mug of water appeared at his chin. Barta took it from Tally and held it up.

He lapped at it and she gave a funny laugh. "Here."

She placed it against his lips, bumping his teeth. Ah, yes, drink.

He drank, and she asked him, "How did you do that?" Without waiting for an answer, she turned to her young brother. "More water and some of mother's salve."

"Here." Essa stepped up to Barta's other side with the pot already in her hands. She thrust it at Barta.

"Tend him slowly—it will afford him his only chance to rest and gather his strength."

Barta dabbed the salve on the raw skin at his shoulders and across his chest. He half closed his eyes, savoring the comfort of her touch.

"The next test," Essa told them, "will be combat. Young man, you have fought before, yes?"

He tore his gaze from Barta's hands and looked at Essa. "Many times, mistress."

"That is fortunate. You will face three opponents."

"Three?" Barta protested, her fingers still sliding over his skin.

"A number, as you know, that possesses significance. Your father will insist upon it."

Barta gazed into True's eyes. "Can you endure this? If you wish to bow out now, I will understand."

"Anything for you, Mistress." He seized her hand

and brought it to his lips, sticky salve and all. She swallowed convulsively.

Tearing her gaze from his, she looked at her mother. "Who are to be his opponents, do you know?"

"Your brother Wick, Urgast, and Brude."

"Brude?" Barta turned her eyes back to True. "He is the one of whom you need to be wary. He's a vicious fighter. Tell me you will be all right."

"I will, Mistress." He wished she might continue to stroke him, touch his head as in the past. But she thought him a man.

He got to his feet and shrugged his shoulders. She handed the pot of salve back to her mother.

Master Radoc sat on his litter, glaring in their direction. "I dare tarry no longer," True told Barta. "Tell your father I am ready."

"Not yet."

Barta took the refilled cup from Tally who stood by watching. "Drink."

He did. Radoc bellowed in protest. "Enough! Let the trial resume."

"Your weapons." With her own hands, Barta fastened the long knife at his side and pressed the spear into his fist before he stepped away to face the three young men ranged opposite him.

Was he to meet them all at once? And would he be able to use these weapons forced upon him? The spear felt strange in his hand, and the sharpest objects with which he'd ever fought were his teeth. But these three young men had trained at arms most their lives. Indeed, this last test must prove most difficult of all.

Radoc called from his rug. "This competition will test your valor. You will battle these three opponents in turn. If you can defeat them all, you will prove yourself and become a member of this tribe in good standing."

True looked at Master Radoc. "Defeat, Master? You wish me to kill them?" He hoped not. He mostly liked Master Wick and had no ill feelings toward the warrior Urgast. Brude would be far easier to blood.

Radoc paled. Mistress Essa answered, "No—defeat means to get your opponent's weapons from him and pin him on his back. There will be no killing on any side—do all of you understand?"

"Brude bared his teeth. "But blood-letting?"

"To be sure," Radoc replied.

Brude grinned. "Then allow me to go first."

"As you wish."

The other two stepped to the side of the ring which had once more formed. Adept at measuring others' emotions, True looked into Brude's eyes and saw what lay there.

Lady, help me.

He had time for no more. Like him, Brude wore a knife, no doubt stolen in battle from the westerners, and carried a spear. Now he drew the knife, bared his teeth, and assumed a crouched stance.

Following suit, True narrowed his eyes on Brude's face—this part of the fight he understood. In his mode of combat one always leaped upward and went for the throat.

Might he use the iron weapon in the same manner? Not giving himself time to doubt, he leaped and swept the knife upward at Brude's throat. The onlookers exclaimed, and Brude raised his knife to block, barely in time. Brude back-stepped wildly, and True leaped again, the strained muscles throughout his body

61

protesting.

A new expression invaded Brude's eyes. "Come on, then," he grated. "Let us see this thing done."

Chapter Nine

Barta's heart, like a little boat on a tumultuous river, rose and fell wildly. She wouldn't let herself question her fierce surge of hope when True began his battle so very aggressively. But when, seeming frustrated with his weapons, he tossed them aside, she joined her voice with those of the others who cried out.

What was he thinking? Was he thinking at all? He fought with an intensity she'd beheld only a few times in the best warriors, all fire and instinct.

Seeing True cast away his weapons, Brude bared his teeth in a terrible grimace, perhaps thinking he had an advantage. But True leaped at him with rampant ferocity, reaching for his throat with both hands. Brude staggered, recovered, and raised his knife in a vicious movement that True dodged barely in time. They circled one another, eyes locked, and Barta's heart rose into her throat.

Courageous and bold True might be, but how could this end well for him? She'd seen Brude fight with a long knife, and terror gripped her. She never should have let True enter this combat. Nothing was worth him risking his life.

Yet he looked calm, hair falling forward across eyes so bright they gleamed. At that moment he looked so familiar she caught her breath all over again. Of whom did he remind her? No chance to tell, for he leaped again, ducking beneath Brude's blade in a movement so quick Brude had no chance to block it. His hands, formed into claws, locked on Brude's arms. For an instant the two men stared one another in the face before True took Brude down backwards onto the ground. With apparent ease he smashed Brude's hands against the dirt, one after the other, until Brude released his knife and then his spear. Anger suffused Brude's face, but he could do nothing except lie where True held him, glaring and gasping. When True released him and both men rose, hate stared from Brude's eyes.

The crowd hooted and whispered. Heads were put together, and Radoc, with a grimace, waved at the second opponent.

Urgast, far more cautious in the face of Brude's ready defeat, took the challenger on next and went down with similar speed. Now the crowd murmured incredulously. Only one opponent remained—Wick, their unofficial war chief. Urgast melted back into the onlookers and let his friend take his place.

The incomer showed no signs of picking up his weapons. From what Barta had seen, his hands made weapons enough, grasping, raking and clawing like those of a wild animal, all his strength focused into his attacks.

Wick eyed him warily and laid his own weapons aside.

This time True did not attack first. Because Wick was Barta's brother? A swift glance at her argued so. He waited for Wick to leap at him, the two circling with their eyes locked, feet tramping the dirt. The crowd held its collective breath, and Barta bit her lip viciously. A few warriors called encouragement, and Wick leaped at last, diving for his opponent's legs. They both went down hard, to wild cheering.

Barta's heart spasmed again, and she feared the worst. Her brother was quick, as she very well knew, and good at wrestling. He'd decided to take True on his own terms. And such a fight could become very ugly indeed. The two men thrashed and rolled together, grappling and grunting. A sudden flurry caused the onlookers to cry out; somehow True had got inside Wick's guard and seized him by the throat in fingers like iron.

Radoc hollered encouragement to his son, who twisted, kicked out, and nearly won his way free from True's grasp. Now everyone watching cried out, most calling Wick's name.

But not all.

Still, Barta did not ask herself where her own loyalties should lie. How could she champion the stranger rather than her beloved brother? And then—just like that—it ended. True, his hands fast at Wick's throat, lifted Wick with uncanny strength and slammed him to the ground in a movement that should have broken his back. Wick's eyes rolled back in his head and he subsided into motionlessness.

Or death.

Barta ran forward along with several others, her mother included, and crouched down.

"He breathes," Essa said.

True, who still stood over Wick, backed off a step. Barta met his gaze and saw confusion in his eyes.

"Winded," Essa pronounced, "and he's struck his head. I hope there are no broken ribs."

True, barely out of breath, bent down and spoke in

Barta's ear. She could smell his sweat—far from unpleasant—and his breath tickled her skin. "Did I do wrong, Mistress? Was I not supposed to win?"

Profoundly shaken, Barta arose and grasped his hand; a frisson of awareness skipped up her arm and stopped her cold. So powerfully did the feeling strike, she wondered if their palms might fuse together. "He will be all right," she said more to herself than to True.

His eyes pinioned hers. "If I have done well, why are you upset?"

She met his gaze again, swallowed and said, "You have done all I might ask, and if I am upset it is not with you. Come."

She led him directly to Radoc, even as Wick stirred and began to rise. Before her father they paused, and the crowd shifted, staring.

"Father, this warrior, now called True, has met every challenge and proved victorious. Will you grant him status in the tribe?"

Radoc, who appeared slightly ill, scowled at Barta and her companion in turn. " 'True'? This is a name you have given him? It sounds like that of a hound rather than a man."

"But true he has proved himself. Someday, Father, he may recall his own name, but until then he shall go by this one." She glanced at the man beside her, who appeared barely winded by all his ordeals. "That is what you wish?" she asked him.

He nodded, and the ashen hair fell across his face; Barta's heart responded with a sharp pang. She turned to Radoc again. "Father, he won fairly for all to see, and you gave your word, which you always keep."

Radoc glared at her. Plainly he had never expected

the incomer to win; this had been meant as a way to dispose of him with honor. Bitterly he said, "There is some trickery or magic in it. How can I trust what I do not understand?" He switched his gaze to True. "You realize should you ever betray us the penalty will be a slow and painful death."

True, his palm still fused with Barta's, nodded again. "I would sooner die, Master Radoc, than betray you."

"Very well, then." More loudly Radoc called, "This man, now called 'True,' has proved himself through trials of endurance, determination, and valor. He is declared worthy of the Epidii."

His hearers went silent, and he paused significantly before he added, "I would so have you welcome him as one of our own." Radoc drew Barta to him by the front of her tunic and dropped his voice. "But, Daughter, you needn't suppose he'll be sleeping beneath my roof."

****

"We must find a place for you to stay." Barta's voice sang in True's ears, all he wanted to hear. Listening to her—merely being with her—made all his hurts fall away.

She still held him by the hand, and he thought how odd yet how wonderful it made him feel. Need dictated that he should have her close; touching her seemed even better than it had in the past, though he did not understand why.

Physically spent from the trials just past yet euphoric, he drew a deep breath of the sweet air mingled with Barta's scent. They'd left the still-milling crowd just after Radoc made his declaration and once Wick had finished climbing to his feet from the dirt, seemingly not much the worse for his defeat, if unhappy about it. Wick moved gingerly as if he hurt, and livid marks showed at his throat.

"He will not be pleased with you," Barta told True before she drew him away. "Nor will he wish to set eyes on you for a time. Come along."

Now True stopped walking and drew Barta to face him. Once more he asked, "Did I not do right, Mistress? Did you not wish for me to win?"

He watched her eyes, as ever, before she spoke. Her eyes always gave him the truth. "Of course. But there will still be questions."

"I do not understand."

"You should not have been able to best those three men, especially after the other ordeals. The fact that you did so smacks of enchantment."

"But it was the only way I might remain here."

She eyed him closely. "Tell me, why do you wish so desperately to remain with our tribe?"

He answered simply, "You are here."

The words did not make her look pleased. Instead she trembled and her shoulders twitched. "All of this," she said slowly, "is difficult to comprehend—from your appearance out of the night to your desire to stay. You will need to give people time. You'll need to give me time."

He nodded, troubled. "I want only for you to be happy."

"Perhaps so, but it is such declarations as that which will raise folks' suspicions. You do not even know me. Why should you care if I'm happy?"

Not know her? He did—right down to her every habit, her every emotion. But he couldn't betray that truth or the Lady might snatch him away, even from this place so hard-won.

So he dropped his gaze and nodded. "I will do my best to afford others time."

"Good. Come with me then."

"Where do you take me?"

"I do not want you bunked with the young warriors; they would make your life a misery. And you heard my father. You cannot live with us."

"Then I will sleep outside your hut."

She stared at him. "With no shelter? Even in the rain?"

What mattered the rain and cold if he could be near her?

But she drew him on into the edge of the forest; all at once he understood where she led him. "You take me to Master Pith."

She paused again. "How could you possibly know that?" She studied him, an almost fearful look in her eyes. "Who are you?"

Ah, and he must be more careful to guard his reactions. He shook his head again. "Do not ask me, Mistress."

The old man had not gone out to view the spectacle—there would be no point in going, for he could have seen nothing, being blind. But when they approached his hut, half submerged in the forest silt, True could see he sat out in front of his door in the sunshine and appeared to have been listening.

For them?

No reason to think so. Pith had been blinded in a battle long ago and now possessed more than a hint of magic.

"Ah," he called out when they drew near, "and who comes to speak with me?"

"It is I, Barta—with another." Barta drew True to a halt in front of the place where the old man sat.

Pith said, "I heard the sounds of a great contest. Have you brought me the winner or the loser, Barta Chief's daughter?"

"The winner, Pith." She hunkered down in the forest loam, and True followed suit. True narrowed his eyes and gazed into Pith's countenance.

The terrible injury that blinded the man had left its mark on his face—a long swath of a scar that crossed both eyes, one of which had been lost and one of which remained, bald and white. The empty socket, deeply puckered, made a stark contrast.

Pith turned this ruined face toward True as if scenting—or sensing—him.

"A young man, is it? What is your name?"

"My mistress has named me 'True.' "

"Your mistress? And who might she be?"

"Barta."

"A strange enough thing, since you do not sound like an infant. Had you no name before?"

True hesitated. Here once again lay dangerous ground.

"He has forgotten his name," Barta answered for him, "and come to us, as it were, new."

True jerked his head around and looked at her. So, she did understand.

He said, "Master, I have been through a profound change of which I cannot speak, and have come to be of service to this tribe. I have just proved myself worthy by accomplishing three feats."

"Why?"

"Master?"

"Why have you come to be of service to this tribe?"

True quivered. He did not know how to lie, barely grasped the art of prevarication, and could not speak the truth.

"My Lady sent me."

"Your lady?"

"The goddess of all."

Pith grunted. "Next I suppose you will tell me you've lain with her, as well."

True shook his head before thinking better of it. "Nay, Master." He'd mated with no one save a few bitches in heat, on abandoned afternoons, and he didn't suppose they counted.

Barta butted in yet again. "He has passed the tests of endurance, determination, and valor, and so Father must let him stay. But he needs somewhere to sleep, a safe place where the young men will not constantly be at him."

"You have much faith in your folk, girl. If he has passed these tests, why should the young warriors harass him?"

"Because he is an incomer. You know what they are. And I said Father must let him stay, not that all here will welcome him."

"So why foist him upon me?"

"You are well respected. No one will disturb your peace."

Pith grunted again. "Come here, lad."

True scrambled forward, letting go of Barta's hand for the first time since the combat. The ensuing wave of cold made him shudder.

Pith reached out and touched his head, an action True understood. The old warrior's palm felt hard and horny, but his touch contained no anger. He seemed to consider what he felt, his face turning back and forth like that of a pup feeling the touch of the sun.

At last he grunted. "Well, he can stay if he promises to help me get up in the morning. It has become a great burden to me."

"That, Master Pith, I shall be happy to do."

Chapter Ten

Morning came softly, muted by raindrops. When she woke, Barta could hear them falling on the dirt just outside her door. She lay perfectly still while the now familiar pain swamped her, the great sea of loss that encompassed the lack of both Loyal and her friends. She thought of the men's lovers, their families. If she hurt so fiercely, what must they feel? This raw emptiness she could not imagine being filled by anything but...

True.

Her first thought of him came nearly as softly as the rain but with an aftertaste of longing.

She opened her eyes and found herself tightly curled on her sleeping bench, an image of True in her mind. Rough and shaggy hair, bright hazel eyes... She began to ache still more fiercely, the desire to be with him nearly overwhelming.

What if he had not done as she bade and stayed with Pith? What if, distressed by his lack of memories and the uncertainty of a future with them, he'd left the tribe as suddenly as he'd come?

Her heart leaped sickeningly at the thought, but her mind argued it could be so. She could not begin to guess what terrible events had befallen him before his arrival, but she knew what had happened since.

She saw again an image of him straining to pull the

lashed stone, every muscle standing out, and her fear increased. Would he stay among folk who could and had asked that of him? But then, would he surrender a place so hard-won?

At that moment, lying in the gloomy dawn, she could not say. Doubt got her up in the still hut, everyone else asleep. She would visit the midden before walking up to Pith's and satisfying herself, yet not let True know she was there if she could help it. She needed just to answer this ache inside.

She crept past her parents' sleeping bench where her father lay with one arm flung across her mother in a gesture of protection. Watching them over her shoulder, she hurtled out the door and stumbled over something on the threshold. She tripped and sprawled out into the rain.

The earth where she landed had at least been softened by the damp. But what—?

Scrambling up, she saw a dark form across her parents' doorstep. It moved when she did and resolved into a long, graceful figure—one of the hounds, surely, she thought. But he arose, and she saw the very man she sought.

"True?" she spat out. "By the lord and lady, what are you doing there?"

"Forgive me, Mistress. I didn't mean to make you fall."

Barta barely heard his words, for he reached out and caught her arm. Warmth curled through her from the place his fingers met her bare skin, an almost painful comfort.

She stepped closer and gazed into his face. "I left you up at Pith's. Safe at Pith's. Why did you leave there?"

He seemed to consider before speaking. His shoulders rose and fell, and he shook his head. "It was too far from you."

What could she say to that? Hadn't she awakened filled with longing for him? Could she deny he might feel something similar and that it had brought him here to lie as near as possible to her?

In the rain.

She stared into his eyes earnestly. "What if the guard had seen you? There are always men on patrol at night."

A strange expression—not quite a smile—crossed his face. "The guard did see me. He came by several times. The first time he wanted to kick me, but he didn't quite dare."

Barta looked around wildly, wondering who had been assigned watch last night. None of the men would be anxious to take True on after yesterday's display of strength and ferocity.

Before she could say so, True slid his fingers from her elbow to her hand, which he grasped palm to palm, just like yesterday. After one instant she placed her other hand in his also, and he drew her closer. For many heartbeats, they gazed into one another's eyes.

Then he said very low, "I care nothing for the guard, your father, or what the tribesfolk may think— only about being in your company."

Barta had to swallow before she could speak. "It should not be so. We barely know one another." But she spoke a lie; she shouldn't know him, yet she did. Could this be part of the magic her mother insisted had befallen him?

True did not seem as troubled as she by the whys and wherefores. He appeared to have embraced their connection whole.

"My heart says it should be." He raised their joined hands and tapped his chest above the heart.

"I know," she whispered in return. "But we can't have you lying outside in the rain." For one thing, her father would never condone it.

She needed a hut of her own for just the two of them. But she would not get a place of her own until she wed. She loved no man of the tribe sufficiently well for that. And anyway, what husband would let her bring another young man in?

A wild idea burgeoned in her mind. If she handfasted with True—stood before her father and the tribe's shaman joined just as they were now—might they then always be together?

"Master Pith says he used to have a companion, a young man who helped look after him, but the fellow was killed in a raid not long since."

"Yes. That is why I thought it well for you to live with him. But if you will not stay there…"

"I will if you ask it." His fingers tightened on hers. "Anything you ask. Just, last night…"

"I understand."

Barta caught a movement from the corner of her eye and turned her head. A man approached at a purposeful plod. Murgen—it must have been he who drew guard duty for at least part of last night.

His gaze skipped over them, lingering on their joined hands. "I figured our new warrior for mad, sleeping out in the wet. But now you insist on standing in the rain also, Barta?"

"We are but talking."

"Looks like more than that to me. You might wish to shift; people will soon be astir."

"Yes. Thank you for…" For not interfering with True, she wanted to say, but it didn't seem appropriate.

Murgen shrugged. "He deserves some leeway after that victory yesterday. If he wishes to sleep in the rain, who am I to object?"

"I am grateful."

Murgen nodded and moved off. Barta tugged at True's hands. "Come."

They ran off into the trees with the soft rain falling all around them while leaves spiraled down like bright drops of gold. The smoke from the settlement fell behind, and fierce joy filled Barta's heart. This felt somehow familiar, running with him, and the way he altered his gait to keep pace at her side.

He felt familiar.

How could that be? Was it mere imagining?

At last she dragged him to a halt, her heart racing, their hands still joined. She saw joy that matched her own shining in his eyes—simple happiness.

"I love to run," he said. "Let us do that again."

"It is not safe to go much farther. Beyond the trees there is a meadow, and beyond that…" She stopped speaking abruptly, Loyal all at once filling her mind. Ghosts lingered in that place. She swallowed hastily and went on, "The Gaels, our enemies, may keep watch. It is not safe." Her fingers tightened on his. "The battle that crippled my father took place on just such a morning as this, soft with rain—he was on his way home with a hunting party and they cut through an open space. The attackers came out of the mist. He was run

77

down by one of their vile chariots."

She paused again as memory possessed her. "Our men got him away—somehow—and carried him home with the rain all running down his face and body. When it dripped off him it had turned red with blood."

True looked away from her at last and gazed toward the meadow, his nostrils flaring as if he scented the wind. "This is a very big land. It seems there should be enough for all men to share without slaughtering one another."

"But we were here first. Since the time of our ancestors' first memories, we have held and loved this land. Our forefathers' bones mingle with the very rock. The Gaels came from across the water and built their kingdom in the west, where it festered like a sickness, spread and spread. They will not share, will not be satisfied till they take all. Who would let another man walk into his home and steal his very hearth?"

True appeared to contemplate that but made no answer.

"Come," she bade once more, "we can at least run back to Pith's. Do you want your breakfast?"

He searched her eyes seriously for a moment before he laughed, a low rumble of sound from his chest. "Oh yes, Mistress, I always do."

Chapter Eleven

"The westerners have shifted their lines, ponies, chariots and all, some distance closer to us." Brude imparted the unwelcome news in a low voice, his head inclined toward that of his tribeschief. His dark eyes looked troubled and angry.

They had met together at nightfall around the fire in the chief's hut, Brude and his small band of companions having just returned from a scouting foray. They kept their voices down in an effort to guard the news—for now—from the others in the room.

True sat at Barta's side in one of the places at the fire, even though Brude had given him a scathing look when he came in. Within reach of his hand, Barta listened avidly and spoke before Radoc could.

"You see, Father—I was not completely wrong when I sought to wound them. Now they have once more acted on their aggression."

Radoc glared at her. "You were wrong, for you did not weigh the cost. Six men dead, do you forget? And your good hound."

True felt pain spear through Barta in response to her father's words. "How could I forget?"

"Then hush and listen. We know very well the Gaels are aggressors and never satisfied with what they have taken. Even a fool understands that. It does not mean we take mad chances."

He switched his gaze back to Brude. "Where are they located now?"

"Just this side of where Barta made her raid."

The others gathered around the fire, including Wick, grunted unhappily.

"Far too near," Wick declared.

Brude nodded. "Any closer and we'll be able to smell their stink." He leveled his gaze on Radoc. "What are your orders, Chief?"

Radoc pondered it, a scowl heavy on his brow. "As I see it, we have three choices: attack them, fall back, or wait and do nothing for now."

Despair flooded Barta—True could feel that also. She said, "I say fight. This is a good settlement, and winter approaches. Do we truly wish to abandon another piece of our land to them?"

"No," Radoc answered starkly, "but potential losses must be weighed."

"We fall back and back," Brude protested, "giving them our land a length at a time. Where will it end? With our backs to the eastern sea?"

Radoc fixed his young warrior with a hard stare. "Would you rather be overrun and see our children enslaved? Or our women"—he nodded at Barta—"used by those rutting boars?"

Urgast, one of Brude's company, said slowly, "Already it is autumn. Surely they will leave off their campaign come winter. They always have, in the past."

"But they will seize all the territory they can before then."

"Not more than they think they can hold," Gant put in grimly. "We are able to raid them in winter and have done so in the past with some success."

"We are able to raid them now," Barta said impetuously, and True's gaze flew to her. "Which is just what I sought to do…"

"With damaging consequences." Radoc verbally slapped her down. "Any such decisions, Daughter, will be made jointly among us, do you understand? No more haring off on your own."

"Yes, Father." Barta's eyes fell, but True sensed no meekness in her.

"Can you not approach the chief of your tribe and ask him to join with us?" Radoc looked at True. "If we are to make a bold stand before winter, before the Gaels take another step onto our land, we will need more men."

Arrested, True returned his look but did not speak.

Radoc continued, "I feel if we can make a stand here and now, drive the Gaels back some distance, we will then have the winter to arrange for more allies and recover our strength. For we know very well that in spring they will come at us again. Surely if Master True returns home and pleads the benefits to all Caledonii of an alliance, his chief will agree to join with us."

Ah, now what was he to say? Had the Lady foreseen this? If so, she had failed to prepare him.

"My tribe also struggles to hold their border in the north."

"Along the Moray?"

"Yes."

Wick looked at Radoc. "Perhaps, Father, it is time we moved north and joined them there."

"You mean surrender? Give up our ancestral lands to the invaders?"

Wick's expression twisted. "It is a bitter draught to

swallow, Father. I am no more eager than you to abandon the graves of our ancestors. But that is perhaps better than joining our bones with theirs before another year passes."

Radoc pushed himself up with a roar. "I never believed I would hear my own son express a wish to run."

Wick leaped to his feet. "It is not the desire to run but to survive. With each defeat, with the loss of every warrior, we become weaker."

Radoc raised himself into a half crouch—the best he could achieve—using the brawn of his arms. "What we hold may yet be wrested from us, but I refuse to surrender it to those vermin."

Wick flashed in return, "Stay here and die then! It is all your stubbornness will win you."

He crashed from the hut, and for a terrible moment Radoc sat like a man struck. In the past, as True well remembered, Master Wick had sometimes disagreed with his father, yet he had never before defied him openly.

Essa approached the hearth and leaned close to Radoc. "What is this, husband?"

"Our son challenges me!"

Essa glanced at the other members of Wick's party. "It is not like Wick to prove defiant."

"He thinks himself ready to make my decisions." Radoc too glared at the young warriors. "Perhaps you all do."

Without a word, the men got to their feet and filed from the hut.

Radoc took it like a blow to the face; he reared back and fury filled his eyes. True, watching carefully, saw Essa place her fingers on her husband's shoulder.

"The two of you are bound to disagree, my love. He will give it some thought before returning and bending his knee to you as he always has before."

"You think so? I think the day will come when he will go his own way. I feel it here, in my heart." Radoc turned his burning eyes on Barta. "And you, Daughter, with all your impetuosity—which of us will you follow then?"

"You know my loyalty is yours, Father," Barta replied. But her fingers twitched in True's like a bird trapped in a snare, and he knew she did not feel as certain as she would have Radoc believe.

****

"What is this? Mistress, what are you about?"

Morning had come once again. True had spent the night at Pith's hut but had gone looking for Barta at once after helping the old man up and giving him his breakfast. He had not found her at Radoc's hut—neither had Master Wick come home—and had searched the settlement for her, at last following his instincts and locating her near the edge of the trees, kneeling.

She glanced at him over her shoulder when he spoke but did not rise. Her fingers fluttered over the objects on the ground in front of her and her distress rushed at him.

"It is a kind of memorial, this."

True looked farther and felt as if he'd been kicked in the heart. He recognized these objects: an old leather ball he'd chased more times than any hound had a right to wish; a rug; and a braided leather lead. All had once belonged to him—when he ran on four paws.

"Ah." The non-word slipped between his lips

helplessly.

She caressed the lead with soft strokes. "These things belonged to one who meant all the world to me."

True quivered where he stood. "A fallen warrior?"

"Yes—though he was not a man but a hound, the finest hound that ever ran beside a woman. Dead now. Gone."

Not gone, True thought, but said only, "Why do you make yourself sad mourning over his belongings?"

"Because his death was my fault. And I could not bring his body home." Two slow tears ran down her cheeks. "I do not know, even, what happened to his body. Did the westerners take it? Did wolves come and drag it away before I could? But then, why only his? Our other dead lay waiting for us to collect them."

True hunkered down on his heels beside her. "Why do you worry for his flesh? That was not him. Surely his truth lay in his spirit."

That made her look at him. "Yes, and what a spirit, bright as the sun. That was his mother's name, you know: Bright."

"Yes."

"Constant he was, and so full of joy. All he ever needed in order to feel glad was my company."

"And why does that grieve you? You were together a long time."

"Not long enough. I ache for him here, inside." She pressed her hands to her heart. "There is a yawning empty place I don't think I can ever fill."

"This hound of yours…"

"Loyal. His name matched his heart."

"Loyal would not wish to see you mourning over his things."

"Likely not." She dashed the tears away with the back of her hand. "But what am I to do with this grief? And the guilt."

"Guilt?"

Again she stared into True's face, her eyes awash with tears. "I have told you, it was my fault. I called for the raid that night against the advice of my brother and others of the warriors. I persuaded good friends to steal away behind their backs. I thought we could slap the Gaels hard, show them why they should intrude no farther."

Her fingers closed convulsively on the lead. "Now they have taken the land anyway. My friends—and Loyal—died for naught."

True dropped his gaze, unable to meet the grief he saw in her eyes—unable to think of words that might comfort her.

She went on wretchedly, "There is no going back and changing any of it. Wick and Father are both angry, and with good reason. I should have lost my own life during that battle as punishment for my foolishness. Instead, Loyal and the others paid the price. How am I ever to forgive myself?"

True searched his thoughts and struggled to express them through the difficult medium of language. In the past he would have thrust his head beneath her hand; words seemed so much harder to him.

"Would he not forgive you, this Loyal?"

Her gaze flew to his. For an instant they connected spirit to spirit so strongly he felt sure she must recognize him. The promise he'd extracted from the Lady returned to him—if Barta guessed who he was, he could tell her all.

But Barta said only, "He would."

"Then I do believe it would grieve him to see you weeping now."

She smiled wanly, pain bright in her eyes. "I do not weep often, I assure you—warriors rarely weep. And yes, Loyal hated it when I did. He would lick the tears from my face."

True reached out and brushed the moisture from her cheek with his thumb. When he touched her, sensation once more rushed through him—warmth, delight, and that wondrous feeling of belonging. The pieces of his life so recently scattered came together for a few precious moments.

She leaned closer to him, still gazing into his eyes. "And what am I to do with this gaping hole where my heart used to be?"

"Get another hound?" he suggested.

"Never. No other can ever fill his place."

"Then, Mistress, you must wait for your grief to subside."

She shuddered, and more tears came. Following pure instinct now, he drew her into his arms and let his lips follow their tracks. She tasted of salt and bliss. He closed his eyes for an instant, love flooding him. He needed only this.

But what of Barta?

She tensed for one brief instant and went still in his arms. He distinctly felt something break inside her before she leaned against his shoulder and turned her face. Her lips met his.

And what wonder was this? A sharpening of sensation, immediate and bright—emotion like none he'd ever tasted. A staggering wave of desire.

Toward his mistress? No, no, and no. He belonged to her, but not that way.

She quivered in his arms, pressed her lips more closely against his, and parted them. Her flavor surged upon him, like that he'd tasted in the past yet a hundred times stronger and beyond pleasing.

Shock caused him to withdraw. Once more they stared into one another's eyes. True felt the silver cord that had always joined them flare and tighten.

"Ah," Barta breathed. Only that one word, but True understood. His world had once more altered impossibly.

Chapter Twelve

"A word with you, Barta, if you do not mind."

The request sounded obliging, the tone harsh and abrupt. Barta, caught behind her father's hut at first light, whirled from her washing to find Brude standing directly behind her.

Another endless night had passed during which she'd lain awake aching for Loyal. This night's torment had a new component however; in addition to longing for her hound, she'd craved True's presence also.

The last thing she wanted was Brude at her elbow, wearing a querulous look on his face.

To be sure, she'd known Brude all her life and seldom found him in a good mood. Intense and serious, he was usually worked up about something and frequently angry. She avoided him when she could and ignored him when able. Quite obviously she could do neither now.

She sighed and laid aside her drying cloth. The morning, brisk and cool, did not encourage standing outside while still damp. "What is it, Brude?"

He eyed her carefully from her wild head downward, his gaze seeming to linger at the place where her tunic lay partially open. Never before had he looked at her in quite this manner—only with annoyance and frequently with condemnation. She shivered involuntarily and, being Barta, returned the stare, taking in his dark auburn hair—pinned with a leather band around the top of his head and heavy with grease—and the bruises he still bore from his competition with True.

"Where is your companion? I heard he likes to sleep at your father's door." Brude sneered openly. "At least so says the guard."

Barta's chin tipped up. "And what is that to you?"

"A peculiar thing to do, especially as he scarcely knows you, nor you him."

"He has been sent—"

"No doubt, but by whom? He will not give us the name of his chief. That is what concerns me."

Barta fastened the front of her tunic with suddenly stiff fingers. "My mother says magic is involved."

"Convenient, that. An explanation that can neither be proved nor disproved. He appears from nowhere with a mad story, defeats a few of us in contest—using trickery, I might add…"

"What trickery?"

"I know not, but he should never have been able to win more than one of those contests. You may be fool enough to trust him. I never will."

"My father trusts him," Barta declared, not quite sure that was true. "Do you call your chief a fool also?"

Brude waved a hand dismissively. "Your father may claim to accept him. After that contest, what else could he do to save face? Do not deceive yourself, though; Radoc is as suspicious as I am." He scowled harder. "Who turns up bearing weapons but no clothing, marked by tattoos not quite like those with which we are familiar yet not quite different, and claiming he remembers not what befell him?"

"You are just angry because he defeated you."

Brude stiffened, proving the assertion. But of course, Barta thought, he could not admit it.

"Think what you will, Barta. But I warn you, do not allow this interloper to draw you in any further."

"Draw me in? I do not understand."

Brude's expression grew still more grim. "I saw the two of you together yesterday, you and your 'True.' "

"Oh?" Barta's thoughts raced. "Where?"

He smiled thinly. "Striving to recall your actions, are you?" Brude stepped closer. "Your father has let you run wild too long, that is plain. It is time you stopped playing at being a warrior, settled, and accepted the place you were meant to have. What you need is a husband who will keep you in line."

Barta took a decided step backward. "I do not play at being a warrior."

"You do, and with dangerous consequences—even more dangerous now that you look to bond with this stranger. Have you forgotten any son of yours has a place in the succession of this tribe? Just so you know, I mean to speak to your father about it."

Barta's thoughts flailed. It would not be the first time Brude had poured poison in Radoc's ear. Might he persuade her father to forbid her from associating with True?

She stared into Brude's narrowed, dark eyes and apprehension touched her heart. "Stay out of it."

"I dare not. Too much rides on guarding this tribe—from within and without."

"Do you think I do not know that?"

"Then act as if you do. Why invite a strange wolf to lie at your hearth?"

"I haven't…"

"Your very attitude toward him is an invitation. Listen to me, girl—your father may have become too soft with age and his infirmities to take the hard path. It may well be time he is replaced."

Aghast, Barta replied, "When it is time, he will step down. Then Wick will take his place."

"Perhaps—perhaps not. I like Wick; he is my friend. But I'm not sure he has the mettle needed to lead in these treacherous times."

Again Barta lifted her chin. "Those of our blood have led for time out of mind. The tribe will not deny the succession."

"And how did your father come to the place of tribeschief?" he challenged. "His father was not chief."

"No, but his uncle, his mother's brother, was."

"Just so, and when the uncle had no living son, the place passed to his sister's son. Remember that. You are not only a wild girl but the possible mother of the next chief."

Dawning horror crept over Barta. What did Brude imply? What did he want? She slid back another step. "I am not sure I understand you."

"Then it seems your impetuosity is matched only by the slowness of your wits. What I say is that I may be willing to make a great sacrifice and take you to wife—for the good of the tribe."

"What!"

"Deaf as well as stupid, are you? But none of that matters—you're a clear route to legitimizing any man's claim to leadership."

"No."

"Be forewarned, I mean to speak to your father of

this matter today."

"You mean to tell him you want to displace him?"

"Not that, but of how I might be persuaded to take you off his hands, troublesome vixen that you are. After the grief you have lately caused, I can only believe he will be all too anxious to be rid of you."

Might that be so? Barta recalled Radoc's anger and could find nothing to say.

"So..." Brude leaned still closer and grunted the words, "trade kisses with your new follower all you like. But I warn you, do not lie with him. Your father will not like it, and I will agree to accept no other man's leavings." His eyes inspected her again. "You are still unbreached, no? Too much the warrior, I am thinking, to indulge in a woman's passion."

The words stung. Barta considered slapping him and thought better of it. His arms bulged with muscle; he could hit back three times as hard.

Instead she retorted, "And what might Wick—your friend—think of you wedding with me just to usurp his place?"

"I trust Wick will consider the good of the tribe."

Barta doubted it. Wick might have his own ways and opinions that often differed from his father's, but he had grown into a capable leader since Radoc's injury.

She tossed her head. "Speak to my father as you will. I shall not take you for husband."

"You will."

"Never!"

"We shall see what you say when your father commands it. Has he risen yet this morning?"

"Not yet."

"Then I will return and speak with him later. You

may rely on it." Brude stalked off and Barta shivered again in the cold wind.

****

"What is it, Mistress? Something troubles you this day."

Barta glanced at the man beside her and tried to ignore her ensuing ripple of pleasure. They had worked together all morning performing chores around the settlement, gathering and inspecting weaponry for the fight that must come.

All that while she supposed she'd successfully hidden her emotions from him. Her heart told her she did not want to involve him in the tangle between her and Brude. Not that she didn't want him on her side. But she wished very much to protect him.

"I am well enough, True."

He smiled wryly. "You are not. In the time we've been together I have learned you like to chatter while your hands are busy. Today you have stayed silent."

"I am thinking about the chances of battle ahead— and how badly the last skirmish ended."

"I see. And why do you keep looking at the door of your father's hut?"

Barta grimaced. Some time since, she had seen Brude enter there; he had not yet emerged. With every moment that dragged by, she grew more apprehensive.

She wondered if she should have taken the matter to Wick, since it involved him so closely. But Wick had gone off on patrol. Should she search him out even now and warn him? Wait for Brude to emerge and try to read his mood? Surely if she and Wick banded together they could put a halt to Brude's plans.

True touched her on the arm, a gesture meant to

gather her attention. Instead it started an immediate, warm hum throughout her body.

She gazed into his eyes and saw his concern for her—that and something more that spoke to her so deeply it made her catch her breath.

"Do not worry on my behalf, True. I have made my path. I must now tread it."

"Not alone. Surely you know I will walk at your side."

Emotion swamped her. She reached out and clutched his fingers; the connection between them flared once more, this time so intensely she had to narrow her eyes against the sensation.

"I know. But the last thing I would do is drag you into danger. I must learn to solve my own problems. I've already cost one I loved far too much. I won't do so again."

True cocked his head, and his fingers tightened. " 'Loved'?"

"I loved Loyal like no other."

True parted his lips to reply but never got the chance. Instead, Tally pelted up to them where they worked.

"Barta, Father wishes to see you. He says you are to come at once."

Barta's heart fell. "What does he want, Tally? Do you know?"

"No, but he sent me special to bring you."

"Tell him I will come when we finish our task."

"At once, he said."

"Better go," True whispered. "I will await you here."

Impulsively, Barta turned to Tally. "First go and

find Wick. Ask him to come as quick as he can."

She straightened and set her shoulders the way she did before she entered battle, strapping on the invisible weapons of courage and determination. She could not let her father or Brude overawe her. She drew her fingers from True's, walked straight to her father's hut, and ducked inside.

Voices met her ears, and she took in also the scent of the fire and the herbs her mother used to purify the air. Her father and Brude sat beside the hearth, Radoc with Bright, as ever, by his knee. Bright raised her head and looked at Barta when she came in; her clear hazel eyes reminded Barta of something she could not, at that moment, place.

Loyal? So it must be. Good to feel him here with her now, when she entered what might prove to be the fight of her life.

Chapter Thirteen

"Sit down, Daughter. We need to speak together."

Barta looked from her father's broad face—nearly expressionless—to Brude's before she obeyed. Brude wore a guarded expression, a man harboring secrets, and her stomach tightened.

Her mother stood nearby, arms crossed on her bosom, and her face gave more clues to her thoughts: she appeared unhappy and a bit stubborn.

Barta comprehended the clash of wills in her household. Her mother, being a woman of wisdom, held a full share in decision making. She bent her husband's ear with her opinions on a regular basis but usually in private and not before his men. Radoc had already lost enough stature through his injury; she would never further undermine him.

Barta lowered herself onto the rug opposite her father and engaged his eyes. "What is it, Father?"

Radoc regarded her thoughtfully for a moment before he directed a measuring look at the young man beside him.

"Brude map Huctus has surprised me this day, Daughter. He has come to me with a request for your hand in marriage."

Barta, unable to feign surprise, instead let her dismay show. She remained silent.

"An unexpected development," Radoc went on.

"But he has made a good argument as to its benefit to the tribe. Has he paid you suit?"

"No, Father."

"Because if he had, you would have done right to tell me." Radoc grunted. "However, I know from experience you all too often fail in what is right."

Barta squirmed unhappily, wounded by her father's opinion. "I have my failings, Father. This I never denied."

Radoc scowled. "Brude, here, seems prepared to take you on in spite of them. What do you say to that?"

Barta turned her gaze on Brude. "I say," she spoke while holding his gaze, "this request of his, come so suddenly, must have some impetus other than affection."

"Of course it has." Brude's voice still held an edge of scorn, or perhaps impatience. "In our world, especially now, there is little room for frivolous emotions."

Barta felt her mother, standing behind her, stiffen. Essa had long argued that love existed in everything worthwhile and made up the magic of their world.

Radoc must have sensed his wife's protest also; his broad hand lifted to rest on Bright's head, and he glanced at his wife before he said, "Then why, Brude, should you ask for my daughter, if you have no feelings for her?"

Brude did not even look discomfited. At that moment, with his dark eyes wide, he appeared like a feral animal crouching beside the hearth.

"I will tell you why." Barta spoke before he could. "Father, he wants your place—he would snatch leadership of the tribe away out of Wick's hands if he can. He thinks he might use my position as your daughter to secure it for our sons, and for himself meanwhile."

"That is not all of it," Brude put in quickly. "I did not wish to speak of this and meant to confine myself to the welfare of the tribe. But your daughter is forming a dangerous relationship with the incomer, whom she calls 'True.' " He sneered. "A name that is quite likely at complete variance with his nature. I still say he may have been sent here to harm us."

"Do you deny that he is of the Caledonii? Why then would any of our fellow Caledonii tribe-chiefs send him to our downfall?" Radoc demanded.

"He appears to be of the Caledonii, but who can tell? Even Mistress Essa says magic is involved. It may be magic worked by the westerners and he sent to learn our secrets."

"Ridiculous," Essa breathed. "If that were so, he would have fallen to defeat in the trials."

Radoc shook his head. "We have laid aside our doubts of him, Brude. His valiance was proven."

Brude leaned forward. "His valiance, yes. Not his background." He waved his hand. "Does that lend you confidence enough to see him in your daughter's bed, perhaps siring her children—children which, if something dire should happen, may one day lead this tribe?"

Radoc flicked a glance at Barta. "What is this he says about True in your bed?"

"She will not tell you," Brude interrupted, "but I have observed the two of them embracing, kissing. She may already have given him her favor."

"Daughter, is this so?"

Barta pushed to her feet and stood quivering. "I have not lain with True or with anyone." Yet. There was no denying the thought had appeared in her mind. "Yes, I did kiss him. His presence comforts me in the loss of Loyal."

Radoc's voice rumbled in his chest, a sound that had Bright looking at him askance. "This is not suitable, Barta."

"If he has been accepted into the tribe…"

"I do not trust him," Brude declared before Radoc could speak. "There is something about him, an otherness. I do not believe he won the contests fairly."

"Other-ness?" Radoc seized on the term.

Now Brude looked uncomfortable. "I do not know how to explain, but only think on it, Chief. How could he win all three legs of that trial without trickery—or dark magic? How could he come here from Moray bearing tattoos we do not recognize? Does he belong to a tribe you truly know? The Bilii, he said. Have you had direct contact with them?"

Slowly Radoc shook his head.

Barta's nerves tightened unbearably. What if Brude convinced her father to send True away? She must speak quickly and prevent it.

"Father, this has already been settled."

"Far too quickly and readily." Brude spoke passionately now. "I say our chief has lost some of his discrimination."

At that moment Wick burst into the hut, sweat standing out on his brow and his shield still on his shoulder. He looked from face to face before he demanded, "What happens here? The newcomer and Tally both came telling me I should get home."

"Allow me to tell you, Brother. Your good friend Brude has come whispering in Father's ear, trying to steal your place."

"My place?" Wick said no more but Barta saw his thoughts move in his eyes. He'd been but a young warrior at the time of Radoc's dire injury and had stepped up courageously to fill a place that contained much sheer hard work and little glory.

"It is clear you are Father's rightful successor. Brude wishes to arrange things differently."

Wick shifted his shield on his arm and faced his friend. "Is this so?"

"Not as she says…"

"He lies," Barta accused. "He has come to Father asking my hand in marriage so he might insinuate himself into the place of Chief."

"Well, Brude?" Wick took it up. "Do I find your knife at my back?"

"No."

"Do you not think I have earned the place and the right to follow my father?"

Brude got to his feet. "You have earned it. But as I have been trying to explain, these are treacherous times, and I am not sure yours is the only—or the best— prospect of leadership for the tribe."

"There, Wick, you see…"

"Hush, Barta." The expression in Wick's eyes kindled. "Let him say what he means honestly, if he is capable of it. You ask for my sister's hand? All you have ever done is deride her for her headstrong nature and tendencies to rash action. Her stupidity…"

"Stupidity?" Barta yelped.

No one heeded her outburst. Essa spoke at last.

"Yet, Son, he understands our laws and knows the important role she may one day play among us."

Wick paled. "You speak of a time in the far distant future, when you and Father are gone."

"Son, we cannot say what will happen, or when." For an instant, darkness clouded Essa's eyes, and Barta's backbone tingled.

Wick burst out, "I do not like speaking of death—it is an invitation."

"You are as tangled in magic as the rest of your family," Brude accused. "We must make practical plans to guard our future against the westerners, and root out any among us who may have been sent to betray."

"So…" Wick threw his head back. "You despise all in the chief's house as you do his daughter."

Brude grew heated. "I do not say that. But sacrifices must be made for the good of all."

Barta forced words past the lump in her throat. "And so he would legitimize his claim on the place through marriage to one he despises. I will not be party to it. Father, I refuse."

Brude spoke to Wick now and not to Barta. "Wake up, man. Our backs are to the stone. The Gaels keep coming, and we do little but fall back and lose men. Now this stranger arrives, full of suspicious motives. I do not trust him and will act as I must to protect the tribe—even if it means marriage to a woman I do not admire."

Wick, looking taken aback, said nothing, and Brude hurried on. "She is just foolish enough to fall for this True's deception and give him the place. She must be taken in hand—do you not see that she, with him, has become a danger? If you are not willing to do it or if you as a family cannot bridle her, I will."

Wick now stared at Barta. "What does he say of you and the newcomer? You do not see him that way, do you?"

"It is not as he implies. We have but become friends."

"So swiftly?"

"He has slept across your father's door," Brude said coldly, "the better to pay her suit."

"I had heard that and dismissed it as fancy. Barta?"

"He did that but once, when he had newly come and felt strange and uncertain among us."

"Uncertain?" Brude leaped upon it. "One who won at combat as he did? Wick, you must feel it—there is something uncanny about him."

Wick shot a telling look at his mother before he replied, "And now who is it bowing to the power of magic?"

"There is magic, and magic. I believe the incomer possesses the most dangerous kind."

"That is not so." Barta too looked at her mother. "Tell him."

But Radoc spoke first. "The gods decided the outcome of that contest—whether they lent magic to any of the participants, I cannot say."

Brude flared, "Just remember, Chief Radoc, the Gaels too have gods to whom they pray."

Radoc sat like a stone, but Wick shook his head uneasily. Barta tensed and turned to Essa. "Mother, tell him he is mistaken about True."

"True." Brude's lips twisted. "I declare it again, he can be anything but." Not waiting for Essa's response, he spat at Radoc, "I tell you, Chief, you must banish him—do it now before he can cause any harm. If you do not..."

Radoc's eyes bulged; he pushed himself up by his arms. "Is it as my daughter says? Do you challenge me for my place?"

Brude did not reply for several moments while a pulse jumped in his jaw and Barta's heart pounded in her chest.

"No, Chief, I do not. Not yet. But I declare I will if things are not taken in hand, if the welfare of this tribe is not put first."

Radoc exploded. "I have lived my life putting the tribe first. I have spent everything I have—everything I am—for this tribe, even as you see me now!"

Brude drew himself up also. "Then I bid you speak well with your children; choose what is best for the Epidii once again."

He went out, and a terrible silence fell. Radoc subsided back onto his rug, his face contorted with pain, and Essa placed her hand on his shoulder.

"Father," Barta began.

"Be silent. Let me think. Leave us for now."

The reprimand and banishment stung. Barta looked at her mother, who shook her head, and shot one glance at Wick, who stood like a man struck, before she made for the door.

Her father's voice reached after her. "And, Daughter, you will keep away from the newcomer, understand?"

Chapter Fourteen

Night spun down through the trees and covered the settlement like a silent spell. True usually loved this time of day when his body tired and his spirit calmed, when he instinctively sought peace. He could remember countless such evenings spent at his mistress's side, drowsing while she sat at prayers with her mother or in the company of her friends, always the young warriors.

Several of those friends remained with them no longer. Through memory thick with pain and defiance he recalled them falling one by one in the battle that had also stolen his life.

And his mistress now possessed no peace in her heart. She'd spoken of missing her hound, but what of her fallen companions? Did she worry about the Gaels even now encroaching upon them, so close he could almost smell their watch fires? Had she become upset during the meeting with her father from which he, True, had been barred?

He wished she would speak to him, but she did not. She'd come out from her parents' hut and almost crashed into him, unseeing. Even now, face bone white and body tense, she barely looked at him, though they sat alone together back under the trees.

He longed for her to touch him, to place her hand on his head as she had in days gone by. Then he would place his muzzle in her lap, inhale her beloved scent, and give in to the deep sense of rightness that came upon him in her presence.

But he could find no rightness now, just disharmony in her spirit—to which he remained attached—and this strange reluctance on her part to speak.

Not adept yet with the use of words, he pondered the problem as the dark deepened around them. All his life he had known her but could not remember her like this, not ever.

He placed his hand on her arm. Startled, she looked at his fingers, traced her way up his arm, and found his eyes with hers. Ah, this he understood—this connection with but a look, spirit to spirit.

They gazed at one another long before he said, "You are rarely so silent, Mistress."

"Oh?"

He smiled. "And I find I like the sound of your voice in my ears."

She drew a deep breath and broke her gaze from his. "I've had a number of things pointed out to me this day, things I should have realized before now."

"Tell me."

"I am not sure I dare. You might turn from me also, like the rest of my family."

Family? Was that how she saw him? But of course, so he was—close at the heart.

"You must know I will never turn from you."

She looked at him again, a searching glance. "I do feel that, yet it makes no sense, does it? I barely know you—nor should I trust you the way I do."

"Is that what they say of me, your family? That you should not trust me?"

"Not all of them. But Brude…" She broke off, and he felt her disquiet boil upward.

"Master Brude is not part of your family."

"No?" She waved her hands. "This tribe is all part of me, no? A greater family."

"I suppose that is so."

"Yet he despises me. And I am not certain but my father and Wick agree with him."

"Eh?" That baffled True. Was she not the most wondrous being ever to walk upon the face of the world?

"How did I fail to see, all this while, how they regarded me? Not womanly enough, not accepting of my role in the tribe, a risk—a danger. I supposed I must be admired for taking a place among the warriors. But that is not so."

True drew breath to speak, to object, but she rushed on.

"And now the raid—that which I precipitated—has only fueled their condemnation of me. My friends, lost. And Loyal…"

She began to weep, something he'd rarely seen her do. Big, ugly sobs tore from her, rending the night.

Helpless, longing to push his face into hers yet not quite daring to, he said, "What of your friend Gant? Surely he does not regard you so harshly."

That made her lift her head. "I do not know what Gant thinks. He has acted so strangely since the raid. He makes excuses to be elsewhere, and I have barely spoken with him. Now that I consider it, I wonder if he does not blame me also, and is just too kind to say so."

"How could he blame you?" True honestly could not imagine finding fault with her, no matter what she did.

"The men we lost that night were all his friends. My decision cost their lives. It is something with which I must live each day forward."

But I am here, he wanted to say. I see no fault in you. Instead he told her, "People make decisions all the time, bad ones as well as good. Your family must understand that. Does your father feel he must pay for the decision that put him in the way of those raiders who crippled him and took the life of his hound?"

Once more she met his eyes. "How did you know about that?"

Ah—pitfalls everywhere! "You must have told me." No lie, for so she had, back when it happened.

"This is different. That just happened; I overstepped myself and chose to launch that raid. I can't blame them for hating me now. In truth, I hate myself. And Gant, who is so honorable and good, must follow his heart even if that dictates that he reject me."

True could not imagine rejecting her. Had he not crossed an ocean of the unknown to be with her?

"You need to see Gant, to ask him where his heart lies."

"No—what I need to do is stop sniveling and feeling sorry for myself, shoulder the burdens I've acquired, and prove my strength—if I have any." She stared away through the trees. "Funny how my strength has deserted me since I lost Loyal. Perhaps he was my courage—and I just never knew it."

True possessed no answer to that. Together they had been strong and were yet.

She palmed her cheeks, scrubbing away the tears. "That, True, is the last of my weeping—I promise it. I must become the woman Loyal believed me to be—the one he gave his life defending."

"Yes?"

She nodded. "I will speak with Gant as you suggest. I can scarcely claim to be afraid of approaching my best friend. But there is a more immediate complication."

He did not like complications. He wanted it to be just her and him, together. But he hazarded to guess, "The westerners at our threshold?"

"Even more immediate than that. Brude has decided he should take me to wife."

"Eh?" True's heart sank violently, and he blinked, not liking the way that made him feel—not at all.

"Oh, yes. He declares since Father and Wick can't make me obedient, he will take me in hand. Plus, it will put him in a favorable position to assume my father's place if need be—if only acting in my son's stead."

"Your son?" Worse and worse. Was that what she wanted? A child? And would she be willing to accept Brude to get one? Desperately he objected, "But you do not love him."

Barta laughed harshly. "Nor he me."

"Do you not believe feelings of affection should accompany marriage?" He knew she did; in the past he'd heard her declare as much to Gant while discussing the tribe's expectations for them. True understood she loved Gant, but she had not given him her heart.

Now, though, he sensed her heart lay in tatters. She believed she'd lost everything, unable to see she had him, still.

"What will you do, Mistress?"

"Well, I will not accept Brude's suit if I can help it."

That reassured him a bit. "And if you cannot help it, if your father orders it?" He could, True knew.

"I will place my hope in Wick. He stands to inherit the place of chief, and has been acting it all this while since Father's injury. If everything else fails, I suppose I must turn to Gant after all."

"Turn to Gant?"

She cast another look at True. "Brude cannot wed with me if I wed with Gant first."

Sickness once more roiled in True's gut. He liked Master Gant, truly. But this prospect sat no better with him than the other. People, so the goddess had said, were complicated—unlike hounds. He almost wished he were a hound again. Right now, he knew only what he knew: he needed to be with Barta at any cost.

And he adored her.

How could he make her understand that?

"Speak to Master Gant, if wedding him will make you feel protected."

"Being with Loyal made me feel protected." She fastened her gaze once more on his. "As does being with you, though I don't understand why that should be. Can you explain it, True? Why does my heart find the same peace in your company?"

He reached out and captured her hands, unsatisfying when what he truly wanted was to lick her cheek. "Listen to me, Mistress. I came here solely for your comfort. How can it be strange if that is what I bring you now? As for Master Brude, it does not matter what he or anyone else says of you. You are perfect as you are. That is how I see you. Understand?"

Her eyes widened. She shook her head.

His fingers tightened on hers. "You must believe that, if nothing—"

He got no further; Barta swallowed his words when she leaned forward and pressed her mouth to his.

Ah, and he had been so hungry for another taste of her. Just as when they'd kissed before, her flavor swiftly possessed him, sharp and intense. His heart began to pound up in his ears and still more emotions—none of which he could readily comprehend—leaped to life in his mind.

This, somehow, made an answer to all his longing, his desire to be close to her and closer still. Better than lying with her on her bed or with his muzzle in her lap—more intimate and far more thrilling.

She whimpered and parted her lips beneath his, which further excited him. She slid her hands up his shoulders and fastened them around his neck, just the way she used to hug him when he was still a hound. Instincts he did not recognize arose and threatened to overwhelm him. He might not know how to react, but this new body of his did.

He drew her onto his knees and gave in to the impulse to lick her as he had so often in the past. Only this time his tongue had access to the inside of her mouth and he took full advantage. She tasted stronger and more alluring, far better than he could have imagined. Her flavor made him feel powerful and determined, almost as he had during his trial—as if he could do anything for her sake.

Was kissing her a kind of magic, a gift from the goddess? If so, he surely should not refuse what came offered so sweetly.

Barta seemed to agree. She wiggled nearer, so she rested against his shoulder, and began to lick him in return, her tongue sliding and tangling with his.

Amazing. Enflaming. Unparalleled in his experience. Those words came to him at last, but not possibly from his own mind. From hers? He could feel wild emotions streaming from her, hot and demanding. She wanted something.

So did he.

He liked this far better than licking her hands or her cheek. He wanted to keep doing it all the night long. Except something interesting had begun happening to him down below—just between his legs and where her thighs rested. Familiar yet ever so different—could this be akin to what had beset him when he followed those bitches in heat on abandoned afternoons?

Perhaps, but ever so much more complicated.

Barta broke the kiss abruptly, and her hands slid from his neck to cup his face.

"True, oh, True—look at me."

He already stared into her eyes with a fixedness that argued she made up his world. He wanted desperately to taste her again—wanted more, truth told—but would be held by her will, as always.

"My father wants me to stay away from you. But how can I possibly do that now?" She laughed unsteadily. "You, not Gant, are the answer. There will be no need for me to wed poor Gant. Not if I wed you instead."

Chapter Fifteen

"Gant, can you spare me a moment? We need to speak together."

Barta's best friend turned his head and stared into her eyes. Having just returned with a number of the other warriors from a night patrol, he still carried his spear on his shoulder.

He halted and waited for the others to pass before he spoke. "Do we so, Barta? And why now?" He looked behind her pointedly. "Strange to see you without your new favorite companion."

"You mean True?"

"To be sure, I mean True." Gant glared at her; she could scarcely remember seeing his expression so hard.

She drew a breath. "You don't like him."

"I don't know him, do I? Nor do you, when it comes to it, but that has not kept you from shifting all your allegiance to him."

"I have done no such thing."

"I say you have. Ever since that accursed contest you have been able to see no one else. I do not deny he gave an impressive show of himself. Nor do I overlook the fact that you are grieving for Loyal." Gant, so rarely harsh with anyone and never one to speak hastily, relented a bit in his fierce stance. "I can only imagine how hard it must be for you."

She met his eyes miserably. "There is the grief, the

guilt, and the blame. Do you also blame me for what happened that night, Gant?"

He glanced around. "We cannot speak here. Let me shed my weapons. Our old place?"

Their old place—the edge of the woods where she had lately taken to sitting with True. She dared not tell Gant that, so she merely nodded.

"Give me a few moments. And come alone."

"I will." As far as she knew, True remained with Pith, helping the old man to bed.

She went by the brewer's hut and picked up two cups of heather ale before retreating to the trees. Gant soon joined her, and she handed him one. He drank gratefully.

"What is the news from the border?" she asked.

"Naught to the good. The Gaels have shifted their camp once again, and still closer. I am surprised on a still night like this we cannot hear them farting. They've also increased in number. How many men do you suppose they lost in your raid?"

"Hard to say. Perhaps eight or nine."

"They will not feel it now. They must have brought more men in from the west. I expect they breed like vermin."

"Ill news indeed." Barta reflected on it unhappily. "Has someone told my father?"

"Brude goes to him now. We will have to decide what's to be done."

"What can be done?"

Gant shrugged. "Fall back eastward, try to join with other tribes farther north." He drank again. "That is what your brother thinks we should do."

She took the empty cup from his hand and replaced

it with her full one.

He grunted his thanks. "So what did you want to tell me?"

"It is about Brude, in truth. He's asked for my hand."

"What?" Gant lowered his cup. "I do not think I heard you right."

"He's gone to my father and said he's willing to take me to wife. He seems to think no one's handling me properly."

"And he believes he could?" Gant snorted. "You'd kill one another in a fortnight—if it took that long."

"What can I do, Gant?"

"Refuse. It would not be the first time you rebelled against what folk want you to do. By the goddess, I should think they would expect it."

"Father has lost all patience—and indulgence—with me now. What if he decides he wishes to be rid of me?"

"And?"

"And lays down his law. I mistrust Brude's motives in this—even if I did not detest him. He as much as admitted to me my only value lies in the fact that my son may one day be in line to be chief."

Gant shrugged. "Men like Brude are never satisfied with their lots in life. I would not put much past that one. Just dig in your heels and keep refusing. Your mother will no doubt take your part, and in the end she has a great deal of influence with your father. Now, if you do not mind, I am tired and want to go off to my bed."

"Gant, wait."

He paused reluctantly in the act of heaving himself

to his feet and looked at her.

Barta drew a breath. "Do you also blame me for the deaths of our friends…and Loyal? Is that why you have been avoiding me?"

"I have not been avoiding you, Barta."

"You most certainly have. I've barely seen you these past days."

"This is so, but only because, as I say, you have dropped me for your new companion."

"I have not."

"You have not stopped by the meeting hut."

"True is not welcome there. The young men do not trust him."

"And you would never consider leaving him behind."

"It is not just that. It hurts to go there and find so many of our friends missing, to know I am responsible."

Gant leaned toward her. "You know how fond I am of you, Barta. We have shared many a laugh, many a sunny afternoon, and more than a few escapades. But I say to you now, as a friend: it is time to lay your preoccupation with your own feelings aside, to grow up from a spoiled child into a woman. Begin thinking what is best for the tribe, not just about how others perceive you."

Barta recoiled as if struck. "Is that what you think of me? You agree with Brude's opinion? And so," she fired up, "do you think I should accept Brude for husband—for the good of the tribe?"

"I have already told you I do not. Wick is my friend, and I am concerned with his interests. By the god's horns, stop feeling sorry for yourself and do likewise."

Barta swallowed hard. "Gant, I know I have my faults. I have never denied that. Do not turn from me; I need all the allies I can get."

"If you are in search of an ally, you would do better to leave me alone and speak with Avinda."

"Avinda? What has she to do with it?"

"She has been certain this last half year that Brude would wed with her, once winter comes. She might have something to say about him asking for you instead."

Barta squirmed uncomfortably. Avinda—an undisputed beauty—had never liked her and frequently mocked her for not being part of the women's circle.

One side of Gant's mouth quirked upward. "Don't like that suggestion, do you? There are some folk from whom you will ask favors and some you will not."

Again she gazed into Gant's eyes, wondering if he had always seen her flaws as clearly as now. Then why had he claimed to be her friend so long?

She sighed. "I will speak with Avinda."

"Humbly? Because she will accept nothing less."

"Most humbly."

"Then I wish you well of it."

****

Even at this hour the hut belonging to Avinda's father bustled with activity, his being one of the tribe's larger families. In truth, they were two families, as Avinda's father had married twice—the second time after his first wife died—and begat a whole new set of children.

Barta, who had never voluntarily set foot there before, stood wondering for the first time how it would feel being forced to accept a stepmother. Avinda, among the eldest children of the first family, must long to escape.

Barta knew she would, in Avinda's place. Even now, at nightfall, children darted about and wrestled on the doorstep. Screaming and conversation sounded from within.

Still, Barta found it difficult to feel sympathy for Avinda, who was as sly as she was beautiful and had a tongue that cut like a knife. Barta did her best to avoid the woman.

Usually.

Now she gazed down at the two little ones tumbling over one another at her feet—a boy and a girl—and asked. "Is your sister, Avinda, within?"

They ignored her. One squealed as the other bit her arm.

Little monsters! Essa would never put up with such nonsense.

Someone stuck her head out the door from inside, a girl of about twelve—Avinda's younger sister. "Why have you come?"

"I wish to see Avinda."

The girl stared at Barta with opaque eyes. "Mistress Barta? Will you introduce me to the incomer who won the contest?" Abruptly she demanded, "Is it true he has no wife?"

A sharp spear of emotion unfurled in Barta's chest. "What is that to you? You are far too young for such an interest."

"I am not."

"Please to go fetch your sister."

The girl withdrew, and Barta stood feeling

unwelcome until Avinda appeared a moment later and stepped out into the gathering night.

"What do you want?" She arched her brows at Barta.

"Just a word, Avinda."

"And why should I waste a word on you?"

Humble, so Gant had said... Barta tamped down her rising annoyance and made her tone sweet. "There is a matter we need to discuss."

That brought curiosity to Avinda's eyes. But she said, "This is not a good time. We are about to take our supper. Come back in the morning."

She bent and chased the two unruly children inside. Before she could turn and follow them, Barta said, "I can see why you would wish to escape this house and claim a place of your own. You must be very eager for your marriage with Brude."

That made Avinda turn back and stare. Her lips pressed together in a tight line, and for several moments she did not speak. Had she heard already that the man she'd claimed had offered for Barta? Not many secrets endured long among members of the tribe.

But Barta thought Avinda did not look sufficiently upset to possess that news.

"What are my marriage plans to you, Barta?" she demanded.

"Spare me a word and I will tell you."

Abruptly, Avinda turned back to the house and called, "I will be but a moment." She told Barta, "Come."

The din within the hut fell away as they stepped off into the trees. The forest—ever present in Barta's spirit, if not her conscious mind—seemed to cradle her and offer strength.

"Very well, then, what is this about?"

"Gant tells me, Avinda, that you and Brude are set to wed come winter. Of course, beautiful as you are, you could choose any among our warriors. I wonder that you've chosen him."

"Do you? You spend your time thinking on my choices, eh, when you are not planning dangerous raids on the Gaels in defiance of your betters?"

Well, and that only enforced the reasons Barta did not like Avinda. She twitched but said nothing.

Avinda drew herself up. "Brude is the finest this tribe has to offer."

"Is that so?"

"Yes, and I will always require the best." Avinda's curiosity had not faded. Her gaze moved sharply over Barta's face. "I did consider your brother Wick; he has attained an important position in the tribe, but he lacks Brude's ambition."

As if Wick would look twice at this sharp-clawed she-cat! Humble, Barta reminded herself again.

She ducked her head. "Oh, Brude has ambition all right, and has been acting upon it. You may be interested to know he's asked my father for my hand."

Avinda's lips parted until she gaped; she tottered where she stood. "What?"

"You heard me. It is a purely strategic move on his part. He cares nothing for me, obviously."

"Obviously." Avinda had gone pale, and her eyes glittered in the half light.

"You did not know?"

"I did not. He promised we would wed as soon as the first snow fell and the fighting ended for the season." Avinda glared harder. "And why do you bring me this news, Barta Daughter of Radoc? We are not friends."

"I want your help."

"Why should I help you, a rival?"

"Because I've no wish to wed with Brude and I am afraid he will try and pressure my father to it." After kissing True, she had set her heart on wedding with him, but turning her father's mind to that would be a difficult task. "These are dire times; the Gaels press us hard. By spring we could be anywhere and in desperate straits indeed, possibly with our backs to the eastern sea, defeated."

"Do not even say such things. Do you not know saying it invites it?" Avinda whispered a prayer before she went on. "You always were an unnatural creature, Barta, spending your time with the men—or the hounds—rather than the rest of us girls. But never so unnatural as now. Why would you turn down a man such as Brude? As I say, he is the best the tribe has to offer."

When Barta did not answer at once, Avinda's expression turned cunning. "Ah, I know what it is—you want the newcomer instead. Which of our young women has not been following him with her eyes since he appeared so suddenly…so magically? He is the main subject on their tongues—how graceful his limbs, how bright his eyes. The strength he showed during the trial, and how he might fit between their legs."

Barta, unused to even thinking about such things, much less speaking of them, blushed hotly. Avinda gave a cruel laugh. "You wouldn't know about that, would you? Rumor has it you've never welcomed any man—even Gant—to your bed."

"What has that to do with the matter at hand? Do you want Brude for husband or no?"

Avinda sobered abruptly. "I do."

"Then will you work with me?"

Avinda hesitated, her gaze now entirely serious. "I will. But the goddess help me in such an unnatural alliance."

Chapter Sixteen

"Goddess, help me."

True whispered the words to the stars and waited for a sense of the beautiful lady's presence. It did not come. Following his death, while he floated in the darkness, he'd made his request to return to Barta—all he wanted or could imagine wanting. Simple it had seemed, save for the Lady's sanctions. He needed only to be with Barta as in the past. That had always been enough.

The truth proved far different. Life as a person proved immeasurably complicated—just as the Lady had warned. There existed layers upon layers of feelings and implications, all difficult for him to understand.

He no longer knew how to make his mistress happy. In the past he had needed only to put his face in her lap or lick her chin to elevate her mood. Now he could still sense her emotions, but his presence often seemed to add to her distress rather than alleviate it.

Had he been wrong to return?

No, not that. Never that. They belonged together; the silver cord still connected them. He need only learn to interact with her as he'd once learned to run at her side or attack a chariot.

He must pay heed to the things that gladdened her. Had it made her happy when he kissed her and licked the inside of her mouth? He thought it had, in a strange and excited way. And it had excited him.

The next time he was with her, should he do that again? The very idea started a hum in his blood.

He glanced at Pith's hut, now dark and silent. True had helped the old man to his bed before coming out into the peaceful dark to wait for...what? The goddess did not mean to show herself, and Barta—

His ears caught a soft rustle—movement—through the trees. Someone approached, and by her step he knew her. He got to his feet and watched her slip like a shadow toward Pith's door.

"Mistress, here."

She checked, altered her course, and came to him. He quested for her emotions the way he used to scent for information on the wind.

"True? What are you doing out here?"

"Pith sleeps and I did not wish to disturb him. Come, sit with me."

She stood unmoving, facing him—stiff to the point of quivering. He caught her shoulders between his hands and she eased somewhat, though her turmoil leaped at him.

"What is it? Where have you been?"

Her only answer came wordlessly as she stepped into his arms. She placed her head against his shoulder and her beloved scent filled him, making everything suddenly right.

Why did there have to be words and complicated feelings, both nearly beyond him? Why couldn't this be all?

He wrapped her tight in his arms and closed his eyes on a wave of bliss. Her heart beat against his, and her palms pressed his back.

"True, what would I do without you? I've lost so much. I've lost everything."

"The goddess willing, you will not lose me." Yet the knowledge chewed at him: the Lady had not promised them forever. And if Barta failed to guess his identity, the spell would one day end.

"I spoke with Gant. Like the others, he condemns me."

That True found hard to believe. Gant always lent Barta his support. He whispered, "Why?"

"He sees my faults. In truth, I am rife with failings. He loved our friends who were lost, full well, and just like the others, he blames me for their deaths. He loved Loyal, for all that." Her voice cracked. "He brands me selfish and tells me to get the upper hand on my feelings."

But her feelings were all: they had guided True for most of his life, made up the substance of his world. He shook his head. "I do not understand. For him to harden his heart against you..."

"The night of the raid, he did warn me it was a bad idea, he and the others. Did I listen? I thought I could prove something about myself. Clearly, I have... I believe Gant regrets he did not go to Wick that night and stop things before they went so far. If he had, our friends and Loyal would still be alive. What wouldn't I give to have Loyal here with me?"

He drew her still closer.

"I also think Gant is a bit jealous—of you."

"Eh?" Jealousy, foreign to the nature of a hound, made no sense to him.

"He more or less accused me of dropping his

company for yours."

"Does he not know I would never get between you and one of your friends?"

Barta made no reply.

"And," True struggled on, trying to express his feelings, "does he not trust me despite my proving of myself during the trial?"

"Few of them do. I fear the trial did not accomplish what my mother hoped."

He attempted to look into her face. "And you, Mistress? Do you trust me?"

She raised her head and looked into his eyes. By the faint light sifting through the trees he saw her confusion, wonder, and belief. "Yes. But it's my heart that trusts you, not my head, and I do not know how to convince anyone else."

"Does it matter what anyone else thinks so long as we are together?"

"No. Yes. It doesn't matter when I'm with you; the rest of the time..."

If he had his way, they would never be apart. "Tell me, Mistress, what I may do to help you."

"Hold me, just like this. I feel such comfort when I touch you."

That he understood, for it matched what he felt. He drew her nearer and ran his hands up her back until he reached her hair. She wore it braided tight, like her emotions, and he used the unfamiliar appendages of his fingers to work at the plaits, thinking only of her ease. How must it feel to have Gant turn from her?

How might it feel if Barta turned from him, True? His very spirit quailed at that prospect.

Barta, motionless beneath his touch as he freed her

hair, said softly, "The goddess is teaching me a lesson, or a series of them. I'm being shown a few truths about myself—and I do not like what I see." She gave a half laugh. "Do you know what I had to do this evening?"

"No, what?"

"Beg Avinda for her help. You do not know her—have not met her yet—but she is the most beautiful young woman of the tribe."

"That is not possible. You are most beautiful." Those strange and powerful feelings had begun flooding through him again. He wanted to touch her mouth with his, wanted to lick her everywhere.

She made a sound of surprise, once more tipped her face up and engaged his eyes. "I almost think you believe that."

"I see only you, Mistress. I need only you."

"Call me by my name. Call me Barta," she requested, and pressed her mouth to his.

As a hound he had lived mainly by instinct. Life existed in the moment and he acted at the impetus of the strength inside him. He'd already learned the life of a person proved much more difficult. But now instinct took over in a rising wave to which he surrendered. Men, it seemed, fell victim to impulses as strong as those of a hound yet far more pleasurable.

Allowing his struggling mind to shut down, he reveled in the feelings that now poured through and uplifted him. He delighted in the way his body and Barta's fit together, how their spirits meshed, and the excitement that lay in her touch. He reveled in the heat of her mouth and the way she clung to him. His new body understood what should happen next; he had only to follow its urging.

People could mate—he knew that very well. His body needed to mate with hers, and he never paused to wonder if she would be compliant. He merely explored her mouth with his tongue, tasted her deeply, and lowered her to the ground.

There, to his consternation, she began to talk again. She broke the wondrous contact of their mouths and showered his face with kisses interspersed with words.

"Oh, how I need you. I need this. I don't understand. It's as everyone says—we scarcely know each other. But I need you here, deep in my heart. Can you explain it to me?"

In answer he dove for her mouth again, captured her lips, and let the rushing feelings fill him. It did not escape him that some parts of this strange body had again become fuller than others. A primitive part of his brain understood that would let him slide into her, become truly one with her—ah, bliss! But she had clothing in the way, as did he.

And by the goddess, she would not stop talking.

Now she evaded his lips once again to say, "Have you an answer for me, True? Can you explain this connection between us?"

He could, but he didn't dare, and anyway, unlike her, he failed to possess the words.

He captured her face between his hands and stared into her eyes. "Hush."

She laughed in surprise. He caught the laugh in his mouth as he kissed her once more, still more deeply, till she became very nearly a part of him.

She tasted so good. He wanted desperately to lick her skin and to slide into her.

"Umm." She breathed the sound and stretched her

body beneath his so that hard part of him settled between her thighs. She became—for once in her life—very nearly cooperative and let him own her mouth with his tongue. Only the stars—and no doubt the goddess—could see them here. Dare he do as he desired?

Barta broke the kiss again but only to say, "Here." He felt her thrust her fingers between them and begin working on the ties at the front of her tunic.

He sought valiantly for words amid the fog that was his mind. "I want to taste you."

"I want that too."

Gladdened, he began to assist her, tearing at her tunic with one hand while he propped himself on the other elbow.

She laughed again, a bit unsteadily this time. "Impatient, are you?"

He did not bother to answer. The front of her tunic came open then, half torn, displaying her two white breasts.

He had seen his mistress naked a thousand times. She'd frequently changed her clothing in his presence, and her body had never interested him. They'd swum naked together; at night she'd sometimes even used the slop pot while he watched.

But now he wore a man's skin, possessed a man's impulses, and by the goddess, he took notice. For a breathless moment he lay there regarding her by the thin starlight while her eyes asked him a question. What did she want from him? Given the buzz in his head, he could not tell.

He closed his eyes against the overwhelming feelings, listening hard to the instinct that filled him, then bent his head and tasted her.

Salty, warm, and the best thing ever on his tongue. In the past he'd licked her often, her hands, her arms, her cheek. An echo of that flavor still existed, but wilder, sweeter. He tasted her throat in a long swipe, his hound's spirit appreciating that she exposed that most vulnerable place to him. He ran his tongue downward. Soft, soft. He could bite but remembered she didn't like that. And the swelling between his legs urged other actions.

"True." Half moan, his name on her lips further enflamed him. He lapped the swell of one breast and she twined her fingers in his hair.

Ah, so good—as intimate as the times they'd slept together, her limbs resting on his fur.

She urged his attention downward, where his tongue found the hard pebble at the top of one breast. She caught her breath, and he distinctly felt her tense and flood with delight.

Her breast—not large—fit nearly all in his mouth. The white light in his head increased and expanded, filling his reality. He hadn't imagined anything could taste better than the inside of her mouth; he'd been wrong.

But curse it all, she began talking again.

"True, True, I want to give myself to you. Completely. If I do…"

He wanted to howl at her to be silent and let him enjoy this. Why think beyond the moment?

But if giving herself to him meant he could mate with her, slide that insistent part of him inside her, he should let her speak.

Busy tasting her breast, he made no reply.

"True, tell me it would not be a mistake."

Could she not put her mouth to better use? He wanted her to lick him in return. But she seized his head, dragged him up from her breast, and looked into his eyes once again.

"If I couple with you, what then?"

Couple? Did she mean mate? He felt afire for that but sensed she needed some reassurance.

"What do you fear, Barta?" The words came to him dimly from a great distance.

"That you will take what I offer and then disappear as suddenly as you appeared."

"I want only to stay with you for as long as the goddess allows."

"And, True, would you wed with me if I asked?"

"Wed with you?"

"Join with me—your hand in mine—before the Lord and Lady."

Were they not already joined? Surely the silver cord accomplished that. If she wanted him to swear it with words, what difference? "Yes."

Again she caught her breath as if he'd said something significant. Then she unfastened her trews—those of a man—and began to shimmy from them.

True's heart pounded in his ears and his mind shut down still further to but one impulse: need.

So efficiently did he block everything else, it took a moment to realize she'd frozen beneath him and a great clatter came from far off—shouts and cries and what sounded like the clash of weapons.

Air rushed into Barta's throat. "What is that?" Before he could speak she answered her own question. "A fight. We are under attack!"

She sprang to her feet and had fastened her clothing almost before True could stand.

"Have you a weapon?"

"Eh?" He gaped at her.

"A dirk?"

"For battle? I need none."

"Stay here and guard Pith."

He drew himself up, shedding his desire like a cloak he no longer needed. "You ask me to let you go to a fight without me? No."

"But…"

"Never."

"I need you here."

"You need me with you."

Once again she gazed into his eyes. He felt it when her spirit relented. "Then come."

Chapter Seventeen

Fool that she was, Barta had left her weapons at her father's hut, all but the dirk she carried always in her boot. She cursed her carelessness as she ran, winding her way through the trees with True at her heels.

She should have seen this coming, should have stayed close to home regardless of how uncomfortable she felt with her father and Wick. Instead, she'd once again thought only of herself and gone looking for True because his company brought her comfort.

What her family and Gant said of her must be so.

Now terror clutched her heart—for once not on her own behalf—and she could not run fast enough. No time left to think of what she should have done. The Gaels had waited for nightfall to launch an attack, perhaps in retaliation for the one she had precipitated against them.

The Epidii could lose everything.

She stopped involuntarily at the edge of the settlement, so abruptly True crashed into her from behind. The scene before her eyes froze her like an icy blast.

Gaelic warriors were everywhere, all iron and fire. They had invaded from the west side of the settlement in an arc, piercing the guard and pushing in with the dreaded chariots. Already a number of huts had been set afire and the flames revealed combat, struggle, and death on every hand.

Barta saw at once she had no hope of reaching her parents' hut to fetch her weapons. Or to defend those there. She must trust others stood there in her place. But the hut wherein they stored the spare weapons stood closer; she had a chance.

She seized True's arm. "Come."

The weapons hut stood wide open when they reached it. Barta nearly collided with one of their own warriors on his way out, who stared at them and grunted before pelting away into the thick of the fight. She ducked inside, seized a spear and a long knife, and thrust both into True's hands.

"Here." She gathered more weapons for herself. "Come."

The main part of the Epidii defense on the far side of the settlement already appeared ruined. A ragged line of Epidii warriors stood there facing the invaders and their chariots, but many had fallen. By the light of the leaping flames, nothing looked certain; fallen men appeared alive and numbers were impossible to calculate.

Barta saw Wick at the center of the Epidii line. Brude fought beside him and Gede on his other hand. Where was Gant? Even as Barta ran forward she searched for sight of him and found none.

Her heart pounded as it always did during battle, a great drum in her ears that blotted out other sounds, even the bellowing and screaming. She spared a thought for her parents and Tally—*please, goddess, let them be safe*—before she leaped forward to strengthen the line with True beside her. She had time only to register how natural—how familiar—his presence felt before her mind narrowed to survival.

Not her first battle but perhaps her fiercest. Gede roared constantly to one side of her; True growled and leaped on the other, the spear she'd given him an extension of his arm. Opposite she saw sweating faces of the Gaels, at least one of which she recognized. The leader with the flying yellow hair faced off against Wick and—at least twice that Barta saw—nearly took him down.

During the following moments, half mad with terror and determination, Barta felt grateful the knot of fighters close to her held and that the Gaels could not maneuver their chariots any farther in among the huts. Many lay dead on both sides before the Gaelic warrior with the yellow hair at last called a retreat. They went dragging their dead with them, some piled onto the carts before they rolled away.

Barta drew a breath—it felt like her first in a long while—and sank to her knees where she stood, her brain screaming. Her ears once more could make sense of the sounds that filled them—words and hoarse commands, the terrible howl of an injured hound and the crackle of flames.

Beside her?

True stood as if frozen, covered in wounds. Part of her had remained conscious of him all the while, but still her relief at seeing him there made the breath catch in her throat. The others?

She looked around and sickness rose to the back of her throat They'd fought standing more or less over the body of Urghast, whose place she'd taken in the line. She'd been aware of that all the while on some level; now she encountered his staring eyes and marked the slash to his throat that had nearly severed head from body.

She swayed on her knees, and True seized her arm.

"Wick," she said.

"There."

He stood not three paces from her, on his feet and dripping blood. Gede, who'd fought beside her? Now, like Barta, on his knees, head bowed and gasping.

She crawled to him. "Gede? You are injured."

He held out both arms like a man in a daze—covered in sword bites, he too oozed blood.

"Where is Gant? Was he fighting with you?" Barta's heart spasmed in her chest. "Did he fall?"

Gede ignored her as if he did not hear. She scrambled to her feet but could not see Gant anywhere. "True," she gasped, "I need to find Gant."

But for the first time, True had left her side. Frantic, she gazed about and sighted him beside one of the felled hounds.

She started toward him, but Wick caught hold of her. His eyes, wide with shock, engaged hers. Blood dripped from both his forehead and cheek, but he lived.

"Our hut," he gasped. "They attacked there first. Mother! And Father…"

"Unable to defend himself." Or his beloved wife. "Tally?"

"Stayed there. Come with me."

Hand in hand, they ran. Barta dimly registered that True, still grieving over the slain hound, rose and followed them. Most of her attention focused on her parents' doorway.

The hut looked far too still and dark within. Wick snatched up one of the flaring torches; they stepped in and saw…

Barta's mind blanked again, unable to accept the evidence of her eyes. Destruction lay everywhere. Baskets and ewers had been overturned; a stream of ale coursed across the dirt floor.

And mingled with blood.

A sound came from Wick's throat such as Barta had never before heard—a grinding roar that screamed protest and desolation. "Father!"

Radoc must have arisen somehow from his bed when the intruders came pushing in. His dirk still lay in his fingers. His lower limbs, hopelessly contorted, showed how wasted they had become. His eyes—very like Urghast's—stared sightlessly and the hilt of a westerners' dirk protruded from his heart.

Across his feet lay his faithful hound, Bright, a snarl still twisting her face. The sight struck Barta on two levels—she loved Bright for her own sake, and the sight of her lying so brought the memory of Loyal rushing upon her once again, paralyzing.

Behind Radoc…

"No," Barta gasped. Now she saw why Radoc had arisen so impossibly. It had been in an effort to defend his wife.

Yet he had failed. They had all failed.

A second ragged sound tore from Wick's throat. He fell first at Radoc's side and touched him with wondering hands before crawling like an infant to his mother and gathering her into his arms.

Essa's head lolled, her body lifeless. Pain blossomed anew in Barta's heart and threatened to choke her. *No, no, no.*

"Tally?" she croaked.

She did not see her young brother anywhere. Not possible that he had fled—cowardice did not lie in the lad. Yet Barta could only imagine the scene here at its height—Radoc striving to defend their home and the raging Gaels, swords in hand.

A sob tore from Wick, who cradled his mother in his arms. "Ma? Ma!"

"Wick, we must find Tally. You said he stayed behind here."

Wick stared at her, a great darkness in his eyes. True, who had gone down beside Bright much as he'd knelt by the slain hound outside, now rested his hands in her fur.

Very carefully, Barta stepped over her father's body to Wick's side. Her mother, gathered against his chest, looked strangely peaceful as if her life hadn't just ended, as if all their lives hadn't just been rent hideously.

"Tally," she said again, this time into her brother's ear.

Wick kissed Essa's forehead tenderly. Ignoring Barta he gasped, "What will become of her wisdom, all the magic she held?"

Barta's answer came from nowhere. "The goddess will guard it, and bestow it on another." A sound caused her to look up overhead for the first time. "Wick, the roof is afire."

The flames crept like a sneak thief, nearly silent, across the top of the thatch. How long before it collapsed on them?

"Wick, Wick!" She grasped her brother's shoulders. "We must find Tally."

"Bring them outside." Wick arose with Essa in his

arms. Before Barta could speak again, he shoved past her and carried his burden from the hut.

Barta turned to True. "Help me find Tally."

He arose at once from his place beside Bright; tears wetted his cheeks.

Wordlessly, he shifted the body of the hound, the muscles of his arms cording. Tally lay beneath her, just as Barta had once lain beneath the body of Loyal.

"Oh, by the goddess!" she gasped. "Alive?"

True nodded, seeming unable to speak.

Barta, disregarding the flames overhead, dropped to her knees. Bright had guarded her master's most dearly beloved child even as her son, Loyal, had guarded Barta, and paid the same price. Valiant, valiant hounds.

"Tally, Tally…"

He breathed, only just. Barta tried to gather him up as Wick had their mother; True halted her with a touch on the arm and lifted the boy effortlessly even as the first bits of burning thatch began to fall.

Outside, confusion reigned on every side. Survivors, many of them weeping, ran and called for family members. Most of the roofs were now afire, the flames having played a game leaping from one to the other.

True placed Tally on the cleared space where other wounded—and dead—already lay. He turned and pelted back into the hut.

Barta's heart jumped to her throat. "True—no!"

He must have gone back in for Radoc, she thought. But before she reached the door he reappeared—not with Radoc's but Bright's body in his arms.

Chest heaving, he set the deceased hound down

beside Essa. Wick stared at him.

"We must get my father. Come!"

Wick and True together headed for the door of the hut. They hadn't reached it before the roof fell in, sending a violent volley of sparks and flames through the doorway.

"True!" Barta screeched. She leaped for his arm and hung on. If she lost him too...

Wick whirled to face True. "Why did you bring the hound's body rather than our chief's?"

True, a storm in his hazel eyes, faced Wick down. "Because Master Radoc would have wished it."

With that, Wick could not argue.

Chapter Eighteen

Weariness, grief, and pain from his wounds weighed on True like the stones he had been forced to pull during his trial. Ever since the attack he'd been moving in a fog, devoid of words to express what he felt. Too much loss, too much hurt. Too much confusion.

His mother, dead.

He relived again carrying her from the burning hut, her fur still warm beneath his hands—beneath his lips when he pressed them against her neck. How her great paws seemed to drag and cling to the useless legs of the man she'd lived so long to defend.

Radoc had been dead, yet his fingers, too, had been curled into her fur. They let go reluctantly when True lifted her away.

Now he turned his face up to the sky and tried to figure how much time had passed since that moment. Time, a strange thing to him, seemed to move quickly or slowly depending on what occurred. It moved quickly when he had Barta in his arms, very slowly indeed when he awaited her presence.

He sorted through the events in his mind. They had cared for their dead—so very many dead, including a number of valiant hounds, mostly of Loyal's blood. After that there had begun a loud argument between Wick and Brude, who had shouted at one another while standing above the wounded. Wick insisted they must vacate the ruined settlement, while Brude accused him of cowardice.

"You are weak!" Brude sneered. "The leadership of this tribe has been weak for a long time. Look what has come of it!"

Wick stepped up to him, nose to nose. "Have a care what you say of my father. He spent his life in the service of this tribe and had the most valiant heart I've ever known!"

The surviving members of the tribe—bruised, burned, and bereaved—stood staring, many of the women sobbing. In the end it had been Gede who intervened, moving between the two men like a small mountain. By then most of the huts had burned; supplies had been lost, along with so much more.

"There is no reason left to stay here," Gede declared. "And it's dangerous. I agree with Wick. Let us gather what we can and go."

The surrounding tribe's members murmured in agreement, and Brude backed down. But True did not deceive himself the matter was closed between the two men. Nothing had been settled. Wick, like so many of the others, wanted away from that terrible place. Brude wanted to prove that his—and the tribe's—courage had not gone down to defeat.

They had moved eastward with children wailing, women crying, and many of the men limping, those able to hold weapons making up a rear guard as they went deep into the trees, the wild places. For most, endurance had translated to blind movement, until the light began to fade and exhaustion overcame them. Now, here beneath the trees, many collapsed where they stood.

Barta suddenly appeared at True's side and interrupted his churning thoughts. "Here," she said, and he blinked at the basin and cloths in her hands. "Allow me to tend those wounds of yours."

She looked as bone weary as he; deep in her eyes lay shock, banked at the moment by necessity. She'd spent a long time, when first they paused, bent over her young brother. Tally bore few wounds, but a lump on the back of his head argued he must have hit one of the hearth stones when he fell. So far he had not awakened.

True vaguely remembered Barta coming to him soon after she left Tally, with a similar request. As he had then, he now shook his head.

"There are others hurt far worse than me."

"All have been tended, save you."

She sank down beside the place where he rested, the basin wobbling wildly before she set it on the ground. Kneeling, she moved forward into his arms.

He clutched her tightly, her forehead against his heart. Her arms stole up to twine around his back and clench him just as fiercely.

"Oh, what are we to do?" she entreated.

True knew the answer to that—they would go on, one always went on—one paw or foot in front of the other until life ended. One did the best possible, held to bright loyalties.

Loyalty meant all.

But he began to understand Barta did not need to hear that now. She needed him to hold her while she wept hot scalding tears that broke from her throat in wracking sobs. She needed a refuge and the comfort of touch.

As did he.

All around them, other survivors moved like ghosts. Many women and children remained alive, not as many men. A large number of the surviving men had spread out in a ring around their new position. Dark so swiftly fell; they would need to stay here for the night.

Barta wept herself into exhausted silence while True held her, offering no words. Were there any words? If so, he didn't possess them.

He had no strength in words anyway. But his hands cradled her, and when she stilled he turned his face into hers and tasted the tears on her cheek.

Comfort, deep and steady. The shining cord between them held strong. So long as it did, he could endure any other loss.

He licked her cheek again, slow and careful. She turned her head, and her lips met his.

Ah, she must want him to lick the inside of her mouth again. He certainly did not mind. The bond between them flared still brighter and strengthened, but she broke the contact far too soon and snuggled in beside him.

"Let me tend your wounds," she bade again, "lest they poison. I could not bear—absolutely could not bear—anything happening to you."

That he understood. He sat quietly while she washed his hurts with water from the basin and tied up the worst of them.

"All my mother's cures have been lost," she murmured as she worked. "Gone in the fire. I was able to gather some comfrey growing here. I hope it will serve. So many injured…"

When she had finished, she once more cuddled up

to him. Passing folk stepped over and around them.

At last he stirred reluctantly. "I need to go join the guard. You rest."

"I will never be able to sleep without you here. Besides, whenever I close my eyes I see—"

So did True: his mother's brindle form, her paws clinging to Radoc as True pulled her away. Ought he to have left her there with her master? Now she lay buried beside Essa, and he needed to put her from his thoughts, focus on looking after Barta.

She whispered, "Do you think Wick and Brude will be able to settle things between them? Will Brude continue to make a challenge?"

"I do not know, Mistress."

" 'Barta.' " She snuggled her face into his neck. "Do not call me 'Mistress.' Surely all such courtesies are swept away."

At that moment Wick came by, his spear on his shoulder. He paused, and they both looked up at him.

"Do you need me on guard?" True asked and began to rise.

"No, stay where you are for now. You can take a later post." Wick's dark eyes studied True closely. "You fought well today. You have my gratitude."

True wondered if that meant Wick now trusted him.

"He's the one who found Tally, as well," Barta told her brother.

Wick nodded. The look in his eyes matched that in Barta's, empty and bleak.

"What will happen now?" Barta asked him. "We have no food and few other supplies, and so many injured."

"And we are low on weapons. If you would be useful, True, I bid you go about among the folk and gather all you can. If the Gaels pursue us and it comes to another fight—well, we need to be prepared."

True once more began to rise, but Wick laid a hand on his shoulder. "Comfort my sister first. She has lost much this day. We have all lost much."

Wick moved off and Barta pressed her hands to her mouth. "I have never seen him like that. In truth, he has been leading this tribe a long while, and doing a fine job of it—whatever Brude says. But I do not know how he will hold up now."

"He will because he must. He has your father's strength as well as your mother's, inside him."

"And me, True?" She gazed into his eyes. "Have I the strength I will need?"

"You always have," he told her. "And you always will."

****

It began to rain before daybreak, a cold autumn rain that added to the survivors' misery. They dared not light fires that might draw the Gaels to them. Barta, who had dozed beside Tally's pallet while True searched out the weapons, awoke to the wet chill and the sounds of another argument.

Many of the guards had come in from their assigned places and stood grouped roughly together in the gray dawn. Barta, sitting up, felt shock at how few they were in number—surely no more than a score of warriors remained from a tribe that had once thrived.

She got to her feet, first checking that Tally still slept and pulling his cover higher against the chill. True stood at the edge of the group, and she went to join him.

Wick and Brude once more faced off against each other. It struck Barta how exhausted and discouraged everyone looked; Wick sagged where he stood, and new lines had appeared in Brude's face. Both wore dirty bandages.

"I say only," Brude declared as Barta came up, "decisions must be made. We need a leader. I call for the tribe—what's left of us—to declare a new chief."

"Not now." Wick turned his head away and tried to dismiss the matter. "Not yet. We have only just buried our dead."

"If not now, then when? Will you let the Gaels surround us here before you deem it a fitting time? Will you act before the rest of us are dead as well?"

A few women drifted up as Barta had, to listen, Avinda among them. Wick flicked them a look before he spoke.

"Could you have prevented that attack back in the settlement?" he challenged Brude.

Brude lifted his head. "I believe I could—at least we would not have been so ill prepared. A stronger guard—"

"You persist in denigrating our strength and thus calling my father weak. But were you not on watch during the attack?"

Anger flicked in Brude's eyes. "I was on the far boundary from where the Gaels broke in."

"And you heard nothing? Tell me what my father should have done differently—Radoc of the valiant heart who gave so much for this tribe, including his life."

"He should have chosen a warrior to lead us, someone who could have kept us strong."

For an instant, Barta thought her brother would launch himself at Brude, his anger burned so bright. Instead a sneer contorted his face. He eyed Brude up and down.

"You want the place of chief so very badly? Take it!"

Exclamations bloomed all around, some of protest and a few of approval.

Brude's voice joined the chorus. "Eh?"

Wick leaned closer to him and spoke into his face. "This has already cost me too much and may yet cost the life of young Tally. I abdicate. And so, mighty Chief Brude, why do you not stand there and tell us how you mean to save us all?"

Chapter Nineteen

"What's done is done." Wick delivered the words flatly, his eyes dull. "Now let us drop the matter."

"No, I will not," Barta told him. "I cannot."

The two of them huddled beside the place where Tally lay, using their bodies to block the cold rain from his pallet. Following his abdication, Wick had gone to see how his young brother fared, and Barta trailed him with True in tow. True, however, had stepped away as if to afford them at least an illusion of privacy.

Barta, having argued long and vigorously for Wick to reconsider his decision, now became desperate to move him.

"What would Father say?" she asked at last. "Him barely cold, and already you throw away all he worked so hard for."

Wick turned his head and looked into her eyes. She shied from the great pain she saw there. "Are you saying the valiant Radoc would be ashamed of me?"

"Not that, no."

"No matter, Barta, for I am ashamed of myself! I set the guard last night. Why did they not hear the attackers? Did I choose the wrong men? Too few? Did I send men who were careless? They have paid for it now, right enough, their throats slit in the dark. Never to draw another breath, sing a song, or love a woman. I have buried Father, Mother, Bright, and so many others my heart has burst. Brude is right: I am not fit to lead."

"Nor is he! Wick, he talks much, but what can he do to save us?"

"What can anyone do?"

"We need a good and sensible head in the lead. He is rash and hasty, and cruel."

"Leave me be, Barta. I just want to mourn my dead."

"So you abandon us in our need? You cannot just hand off the place of chief, Wick. That is not how it is done."

"How is it done, Barta? Do we continue to beat our heads against the stone and watch those we love bleed? If Brude wants the ill-begotten place, I say let him take it."

"What of my sons, who should be chief after you and Tally?"

He looked at her dully. "You have no son and may never do, if the Gaels have their way. We must let the future look after itself."

"Father would be appalled."

"I am not the man Father was. Can you not see that, Barta? I have always known it for truth. Now, with everything at risk, it's time for me to admit it."

"So you mean to take orders from Brude? Follow him like a meek hound pup?"

"We have already lost all Father tried so hard to hold. What matter my opinion of myself as compared to that?"

"Carrying on in his place matters, as does the welfare of the tribe."

Slowly, Wick shook his head. "As soon as I am sure Tally will survive, I mean to light out from here."

The breath seized in Barta's lungs. "So you truly will abandon us?"

"What 'us,' Sister? Can you not see this tribe is in ruins?"

"The folk left are still our responsibility."

"The heart of the tribe is gone. It died with Father, with Mother. Let Brude try to salvage what is left."

Barta scrambled to her feet and stood looking down at her brother in disbelief. How could her world come apart so swiftly, and so completely?

"What about me?" she cried like the young child she knew, in her heart, she could no longer afford to be. "And Tally? Would you leave us here, subject to Brude's whim, without you?"

Wick laid a hand on Tally's brow. "Barta, you have long sought to make your own way. This will be your chance."

"Not much of a chance, is it? Where will you go?"

"As far as my legs will carry me. North, perhaps."

"And do what?"

Again his eyes met hers. "Lose myself."

"Go to die, you mean? To waste away like an afterthought of the man you were? That is the worst betrayal of all."

"Stand and shout at me all you wish, Sister. You will not move me."

Barta hadn't realized she'd been shouting. She closed her lips and glanced at True, who stood not far off, his shoulders hunched against the rain. Again she sought for some words that might turn her brother's mind.

"Do not make this decision now," she begged quietly. "Wait for the pain to ease. Wait till Tally wakes."

"The pain will not ease. But, Sister, if it satisfies you, I will wait until morning."

"Thank you, Wick. But nothing about this satisfies me."

****

"Come and lie in my arms." True drew Barta closer beneath the boughs of the tree under which they sheltered. Night had fallen like a thick blanket and the rain had eased, though the damp chill persisted. They still dared not light a fire, and Barta had wrapped Tally—who hadn't yet awakened—close against the wet.

A poor encampment at best, but Brude had set guards all around, making a point of skipping over True for the duty, demonstrating his distrust.

True supposed he should mind the slight, but he felt too grateful for being at Barta's side with leave to watch over Tally, who lay so still.

In truth, the whole encampment seemed uncannily still. Say what Barta would about Brude, he'd impressed the importance of silence on the remaining tribesfolk. Even the guard made no sound.

Barta planted the flat of her hand on True's chest and whispered into his ear, "Do you think there's any chance of persuading Wick to stay? I sent Gant to speak with him—to no avail."

At least Master Gant had survived the battle, though Barta's friend had been found severely wounded and badly burned after being trapped beneath a collapsed roof. Like most of the others, he wore a look of shock and did not appear fit to persuade anyone of much.

"True, I have been thinking—perhaps Tally and I should go with Wick, wherever he goes."

True stiffened. "Without me, do you mean?"

"No, of course not. Wherever I go, you go also. Tell me that's so."

"Wherever you go, I go."

She pressed her forehead to his and held on to him tight, like a drowning woman. "What would I do without you, True? You are the one comfort left to me. And such a comfort! Tell me how it is I feel better—as if I can breathe—just because I'm near you."

He could explain it; he dared not. "Does it matter? We are together; that means more than anything."

She nodded brokenly. "And, True, will you provide me any sort of comfort I need this night? If I ask you to love me, will you?"

"I do love you. You know that. Not just this night: always."

She made a sound, half gasp and half sob. "And forever?"

"There is only forever for us, Mistress."

"Barta."

"Barta."

She pressed her open mouth to his and the taste of her flooded upon him. He growled deep in his throat and gathered her into his arms, onto his knees. In the wet darkness, her mouth became a single point of comfort so strong it lifted him from his misery. He needed no more than this.

She sighed and tasted the inside of his mouth with her tongue. Her hand burrowed beneath his tunic and pressed against his bare skin. Bliss streamed to his head and even memory faded away.

But she broke the kiss almost at once and said raggedly, "I want to touch you, but it seems wrong…so much loss, so much death. How should we take our pleasure amidst that?"

"How should we not? Life is of the moment—only that. Here, and then gone so swiftly. We must take what we need."

"Perhaps you are right." She pressed her mouth to his again, licked him deeply. Her hand took a decided turn downward and warmth spread through him in the wake of the bliss, followed by sharp desire.

He wanted—but he possessed no words at all.

Her fingers encountered the laces on his leggings, paused, and wiggled beneath. His whole body leaped to attention—wounds, aches, and even sorrow forgotten. She curled her fingers around the part of him she sought, and he stiffened. Feelings, raw and hot—so different from those of a hound—poured through him. He wanted to mate with her. Would she be receptive?

As a hound, he'd never had any doubt, could tell by scent as well as behavior when a bitch would accept him. This baffled him—emotions and impulses all tangled together, and his need to protect her at all cost. Even from his desires?

She murmured and began to caress him with her hand. Enflamed, he contemplated flipping her over and completing the act that should be so simple but was not. Confusing him further, she showered his face with little kisses and began to whisper in the darkness.

"True, tell me everything will come right—lie to me if you have to. Say that we will heal, that we'll defeat the westerners, that Tally will awaken and you and I will never lose each other."

His throat closed beneath the lash of his emotions; her hand remained inside his leggings, closed around him in a caress. He had no words.

"Because of all things, I could not bear to lose you too." As she spoke, he tasted her tears on his tongue. "Not after my parents, so many of our friends...and Loyal."

"Loyal," he struggled to tell her, "would not want you to mourn him so deeply." Of this at least he was certain. "There is nothing he would not have done for you, given for you."

"How can you say that? You did not know him."

"He was your hound. He could feel no anger. And he loves you still."

She began to weep in earnest.

"No," he bade her. Using his fingers, he wiped the tears from her cheeks, captured her lips with his, and slid his tongue into her mouth again.

He needed to make her feel how completely they remained bound to one another—that nothing could ever truly part them even if his body perished again. Or if hers did. That thought caused such pain in his heart he could scarcely breathe, and he felt for the first time the truth of what she'd felt when she lost Loyal. When she lost him.

Desire it as he may, the Lady had not promised to leave him with her forever. Their only "forever" consisted of the shimmering cord that bound them spiritually.

But for now, they lay close enough to make one flesh. The last time they had come this close to mating, the Gaels had attacked. Did she want him now? Would it bring her the comfort she craved?

She moaned; True thought he heard the sound echo in the still night. With his senses and emotions both overloaded, it took him a moment to grasp the truth. He tumbled to it a moment after Barta stiffened in his arms and pulled away from him.

"Tally!" she breathed. "Thank the good lady—he wakes."

Chapter Twenty

Barta knelt on the damp ground, afraid to take her eyes from her young brother's face. Tally had come around, groaning with the ache in his head and with his thoughts foggy. The true pain found him when his memory of the fight in the hut returned. He threw himself into Barta's arms then and howled like a young child, while the other tribe members gathered around, silent. Barta had wept with him.

Now dawn crept through the trees like cold mist, and she felt a different woman from the one she'd been just yesterday—transformed like metal when it passes through the fire. Once, she'd believed the loss of Loyal the worst thing she could bear, then the loss of her parents. Tally had returned to her miraculously, but now she must watch as Wick said goodbye to both of them.

Tally, still impossibly pale and with dark smudges for eyes, clutched her hand and stared at his older brother with raw disbelief. Barta tore her gaze from him at last and focused on Wick also. He wore a slender pack on his back and weapons on his shoulder. Even as she watched, he hunkered down at Tally's other side and touched the boy's arm.

Wick's eyes might still be blank, as they'd been since the death of their parents, but Tally's held enough agony for all of them to share. He struggled to sit up, and Wick steadied him with careful hands. Behind Barta stood True, utterly silent, and beside True a heavily bandaged Gant, his face twisted with distress. Barta had no doubt other tribe members listened. She no longer cared if they did.

She—and Tally—had only moments to change Wick's mind and persuade him to stay. The matter seemed so simple to her, despite—or perhaps because of—all the changes.

She spoke impulsively. "Wick, you cannot go."

"Cannot." Tally repeated the word, his voice still raw from weeping. He and Wick had always been close. Surely, surely Barta told herself, he could change Wick's mind.

Wick moved his hand from Tally's shoulder to his hair, which he stroked the way Barta used to stroke Loyal, with visible love. "I must. Now that I know you have awakened and will recover, Tally, I can."

"But what of Father's place? He is…gone. But he left you behind, and that is what he would want."

Wick glanced at Barta once before returning his gaze to Tally's face. "That place can be filled by another—has already been filled by another. Did Barta not tell you?"

Confusion washed over Tally's face. "She has told me much. I don't believe it—I don't care what Brude thinks he might do. Stand up to him. Challenge him. Father would."

For the first time, pain wracked Wick's features, a crack in his stoic emotionlessness. "I am not Father. That is something no one ever understood."

Tally argued it, and Barta heard her mother's words in his mouth. "You are the son he loved and raised. Do him honor now."

Wick contemplated it, head bowed, and Barta dared to hope he might stay after all. But he shook his head again. "I wish I did not have to disappoint you, Brother. I must have time to think, to regain myself."

From beside Barta, Gant spoke. "Do you say you may return?"

Wick's eyes found him. "I may."

Gant scowled. "It will be too late by then. Already Brude takes the chief's cloak upon his shoulders. Whether you do or do not return, he will ruin us."

"Ah, Gant my good friend, we are already ruined. Do you not see that?"

"So," Barta said bitterly, "it will be you and not the Gaels who thrusts the final dirk in our backs. What would Father say to that, I ask you?"

"He would be ashamed of me. I am ashamed of myself. Perhaps, Sister, you were right after all with your rash intentions and daring heart. You should have been the heir to the place instead of me."

"No, Wick. No." Leaning across Tally, Barta embraced Wick, squeezed him tight enough to hurt, thinking maybe if she held on he wouldn't go from them. For an instant their pain, with Tally's, twisted together. Then he set her from him gently and rose to his feet in the misty dawn.

"I am not worthy of the tribe, not as I am. Take care of yourself, Sister. Take care of Tally." He bent again to embrace the boy and clasped arms with Gant, who stepped forward. Barta, feeling hollow, rose to her feet and stood swaying. True took her arm and steadied her.

"This is a mistake," Gant said. "Wick, will you put

yourself ahead of the tribe?"

"Gant, I have not thought of myself in longer than I can remember. Ever since Father's injury it has been harder and harder. Have you any idea how it feels trying to live up to something—someone—you know you can never match?"

"You need not match your father," Gant grumbled. "Few could. Only be the man you are, and that will be good enough for those of us who value you."

Again, Wick shook his head. "I am sorry. I wish you all the best; I pray to the Lord and Lady you find a safe place under their protection."

Gant grunted. "Much good that may do us now!"

From the corner of her eye, Barta saw Brude walk up. To be sure, she hadn't expected him to stay clear of this scene. But she saw only sorrow and no gloating in his face.

To Wick she said, "Where will you go?"

He shrugged. "North, as I said. As far away from the wretched invaders as I can get." His features writhed. "I hate them. I know Mother taught us not to hate, but my feelings have gotten beyond me. If I do not leave now, do not breathe free air, I will lose myself."

Disregarding the listening Brude, Barta said, "You will return when you can?"

"I will. But I am hoping to find a place away from all this death and pain." His eyes lit for the first time. "Come with me, Barta—you and Tally."

Barta considered it even as the others watched and listened. A tempting offer—to flee all the heartache and sorrow. But Wick said nothing of True, and she would go nowhere without him. Sadly, she shook her head.

"I will not abandon Father's fight."

Wick took a measured look at Brude, not ten paces away. "Then stand and make a challenge for the place of chief. It is what you've always wanted, in your heart."

Barta, too, shot a look at Brude, whose expression had become stormy as the sky overhead. "All I ever truly wanted was respect. I seem to have achieved just the opposite."

Wick clasped her arm again. "Sister, your race is not run."

He pushed past her then and paused by Brude, his life-long companion. "Look after them in my stead. And the goddess help you if you fail them."

"As you fail them?" Brude jabbed. Suddenly he relented. "Wick, stay. You need not serve as chief—I will accept that place. You still have much to offer: a good right arm, a sound heart, and strength of belief."

Wick gave a rough laugh. "You think my heart still sound? With such poor judgment, you are all doomed." He looked at Barta again. "I'm sorry."

The last words she would ever hear from him? She feared so, and felt another crack join those already threading through her heart, making of it a poor and leaky vessel.

Impulsively, she leaped forward and embraced him again. For an instant he hesitated, then clasped her painfully tight.

"Stay, please," she begged in his ear.

"Forgive me. I cannot."

He released her and, all in one movement, turned and walked away. Within moments he had dissolved into the mist between the trees, like nothing more than a dream.

****

"Barta, we must speak together—reasonably, if we can manage it."

Barta, the emptiness in her heart like a living presence, made no response. Following Wick's departure, Brude had stomped off across the camp, leaving her to comfort Tally as best she might. Not until now, sometime later, did he return and pause above Tally's pallet to regard her.

True, sitting beside her, shoved to his feet as if prepared to intervene, but Barta held up a restraining hand. Brude appeared changed, and not just because of the wounds he bore. He looked older, honed and exhausted. A different man from the confident, cocksure one she'd come to know.

Yes, well, they had all been altered, had they not? Her mind flinched from the darkness in her spirit even as she used True's hand to scramble to her feet. She strove to answer Brude in kind.

"And without hostility?"

That brought Brude's dark gaze to hers. "Without hostility." He waved an arm, encompassing both Tally and the forest around them. "There is no room left for it."

"Barely room left," she pronounced, "for living."

"We agree then—for once."

Barta nodded and shivered. When she began agreeing with this man, she must indeed worry. She glanced at True, who stood with concern bright in his hazel eyes, and nodded. "Stay with Tally, please. I will be but a few moments."

She stepped away with Brude, who cupped her elbow in his hand. Barta wanted to pull away but had

161

not the strength. She could not recall when she had been so tired.

Brude searched her face before he spoke in a low, steady tone. "I will be as brief and as honest as I can. I want the place of chief. After all that's happened, I scarcely know why, save that I have always wanted it."

Barta drew breath against the despair that filled her heart. "It should be easy for you—has not Wick just placed it in your hands?"

Brude scowled bitterly. "Easy? Nothing about this is easy." He shook his shaggy head, and she saw that a hairline cut along his forehead still oozed blood. He looked nearly as beaten as she. "I need to know, Barta, that you will not obstruct me."

"Me? How?"

"By challenging me for the place, as Wick suggested."

She gave a wild laugh. "That was nonsense. How would I do so? I have no sons."

"Not yet." Brude shot a glance back to where True still stood with his gaze resting on them. "But I know what you are—unpredictable and obstructive just for the sake of it. This, Barta, is no time to play games. We are driven down...very nearly defeated. Our people need guidance, strength and hope, if they are to survive."

Barta blinked at him in surprise. It had never occurred to her that Brude, with all his bluster, might have the makings of a good chief, yet his words made sense.

He went on softly, "I know you. Proving yourself has always been at the back of your mind. Why else did you challenge so many of your father's and Wick's decisions? Why undertake that disastrous raid behind everyone's back unless you wanted to prove something? Your own father stood in the way—and your brother. No more." He lifted his chin. "Now I stand in your way."

She shook her head, thinking the past but a dream. "I wanted only respect—and to prove I might fight as well as any man of this tribe."

Brude did not look convinced.

"Brude, if I did challenge you for the place of chief, do you suppose the tribe would take me seriously?"

"I do not know. Folk are shattered, and the majority of them are women. They followed your father a long time."

"I don't want the place." Once, perhaps—if only as he said, at the back of her mind. Now? No.

"What of your companion?"

"Who? True?"

"An absurd name—better suited to a hound than a man. I do not trust him, but I can see you do and thought you might be grooming him for your consort— a strong spear at your side to persuade the tribesfolk of your might."

"That is not uppermost in my mind."

Brude grunted. "I may not trust him, but by the goddess, he's fearless in a fight, and at the moment that counts for something. If you do not mean to take him for husband, then hear me out—and patiently. I say again, it is time for us to put the welfare of this tribe first and make choices to benefit them—not ourselves." His gaze narrowed upon her. "I still think you and I should wed."

Barta drew breath to speak but he forestalled her. "Nay—we agreed to speak honestly, so listen. I do not want you—I am certainly not attracted to you. I think but of the tribe. Our folk need healing, and they need to believe in those who lead them. If we wed, they will see you—a member of your father's house—giving me your backing. And our children would still carry that bloodline."

"Children?" she gasped in horror.

"I think of the future, Barta, nothing more. I know you for a selfish wretch, right down to your toes. But will you not for once join me in acting on behalf of someone besides yourself?"

Dismay washed over Barta in a wave; she felt far too weary to experience affront. Again she drew a breath. "This is not the time for such decisions. We have far greater worries—no food, no fire, many injured and bereaved, and winter coming on."

"Leadership comes first, always."

She crossed her arms on her breast. "Very well—as chief, what is the first thing you would do?"

"Move us east."

"But are you not the man who decried Wick's decision to fall back, who branded us cowards if we ran?"

Brude blinked. "Much has changed since then. Many whom we loved have gone into the ground. I am not sure we have warriors enough to stand, should the Gaels pursue us."

"So you would move us east. Why not north, where we might find some allies?"

"The tribes due north of us are fighting their own battles. And your erstwhile champion will not cough up

164

the name or location of his folk." Brude's nostrils flared.

"He cannot remember. He suffered a life-changing event…"

"So you keep saying. Yet he remembered he was supposed to come and place himself in your service."

"Mother said there was great magic in it."

"No doubt. And it no longer matters. Wed with me and you can keep him on the side."

"Eh?"

"I mean to speak with Avinda about a similar arrangement."

Barta stared. "Do you truly suppose Avinda will accept you without the title of wife?"

"She will do what is best for the tribe."

Barta doubted that. "But…would she not want your children?" Heat stained Barta's skin. She hated speaking of such things with Brude and did not want to imagine lying down with him.

"She must be made to understand—as must you—that the only issue that matters would be our children, yours and mine. Is that not the whole point of us marrying? Which means," he jerked his head toward where True still stood, watching, "should you take him to your bed, your children cannot be his." Brude's gaze raked her. "Even a poor excuse for a woman such as you must know of other ways you can pleasure him, and he you. Or are you entirely the warrior lad?"

Barta's cheeks now burned, but she tipped up her head. "I do not wish to wed with you—not for any reason."

"Nor I you. Sacrifices must be made, especially now. Just say you will consider on it—and that you will support me in the meantime as chief."

Barta narrowed her eyes and tried to see into a future that appeared to contain only darkness. She sighed. "Very well, Brude. I will consider on it, no more."

Chapter Twenty-One

All day they tramped through the silent, soaking forest, carrying their wounded and the scanty belongings they still possessed. True, a pack of goods slung across his back, toted the rear of Tally's litter, with Barta at the front. The lad had tried to walk on his own, but weakness overcame him.

Barta said little, and her face remained tense and white. Since her conversation with Brude, True barely recognized her mood, and her aura had turned dark gray. But she continued to trudge on, following Brude, who led them all, Avinda at his side.

They moved quietly for so many, especially with wounded and babies among them, and paused only now and then to rest. True's wounds stung badly, and he worried about those Barta carried. Yet she never faltered until Brude at last called a halt, late in the day.

By then the rain had ceased and the sky cleared. Far behind them to the west, the sun set in fiery bands of orange and red. Folk set down their burdens, groaned, and whispered together.

Brude immediately set about assigning a guard. He called upon Gant and several others of the surviving warriors but once again bypassed True.

On his way back through the ragged crowd, Barta stopped him. "You have not assigned me. Or True."

Brude's gaze flicked over them. True saw that his

aura, too, had damped down from its usual hues, which had more or less matched the sunset.

"I thought you would sooner have leave to look after Tally."

"We are willing to do our part."

"I think I have enough men for now."

Barta reached out as if she would touch Brude's arm and withdrew, thinking better of it. "You do not trust me?"

"He does not trust me," True spoke softly. It didn't matter to him either way. He needed only to be at Barta's side.

Moderately, for him, Brude said, "We are all learning a new path through this darkness."

"He is trying," True told Barta once Brude moved on.

"I am too weary to worry at it."

"Let us get Tally settled and comfortable. Then you can help tend the wounded—once we see to your hurts, that is."

"I am well enough."

True engaged her eyes and held them. "You are not."

"True, I will not allow myself to come first—not again. Those days are over."

"You always come first with me, Barta. Understand?"

He saw and felt emotion whip through her. Tears filled her eyes, and she nodded.

"You must be hurting also. You fought like a wolf back there."

"Come, do not worry about that now."

Barta fretted softly the whole time they tended

Tally together, expressing her worry about the trail so many feet must have left through the wet forest, and how they could hope to make Tally comfortable in the waning light. Indeed, by the time they finished, the sunset's last radiance had slipped away; cold, damp dark came down.

Barta went off then, moving from group to group. Folks had more or less settled wherever they stood when Brude called a halt, and she stooped down at each place, offering what assistance she could. True knew she carried a measure of Essa's knowledge, but all her mother's supplies had been lost, turned to ash.

At the thought, an ache started in True's heart. A hound did not carry sorrow as such, though he might continue to long for those gone. Now True began to realize he was no longer just a hound. He'd been raised from a pup in Radoc's household—Barta's family, as much as Bright and his littermates, was his pack. He felt hollow, pain rushing in as shock faded.

He heard a sound close at hand, and a shadow shifted. "Where is Barta?"

Gant, with his spear on his shoulder—part of the guard Brude had posted.

"Lending a hand where she may."

Gant grunted. True heard doubt in the sound, and unhappiness. "How does Tally fare?"

"Sleeping now. He remembers something of the attack, recalls Bright throwing herself over him. We had to tell him neither of his parents survived." True hesitated. "I think Barta fears he will lose himself in his grief and choose not to return to us."

"Look after him. And after Barta also, will you?"

Gant moved off again before True could reply. He

169

sank down on his haunches, thinking hard, and placed a protective hand on Tally's chest; the boy lay so silent. As a hound, he hadn't indulged much in deep thought. Things were as they were and patience had been built into his nature. Now his heart pricked and worry niggled at him.

"Master True?"

The whisper came at him out of the dark. One—no, two more shadows stirred. He could smell they were young women, friends of Tally's.

They both crowded close. "How is he?" asked one.

True answered gently, "He awakened for a while but has drifted off again."

"Perhaps if we were to sit with him, speak to him?"

"Yes, but softly now. You know how sound carries in the dark."

The second girl asked, "Do you think the Gaels will pursue us?" She shivered, and True guessed what lay in her mind. Girls her age—not above fourteen— might be seized and treated without mercy. Slaves, they could become open to every sort of abuse.

"I do not know," he told her honestly.

The girls sat close beside Tally. One of them traced his brow with her fingers. "He is so handsome. With Chief Radoc dead and Master Wick gone, do you think Tally will take up the place of chief?"

"Master Brude has stepped into that place," True reminded the girl who had spoken.

"Yes, but my father says that is not right, that someone of Radoc's blood should be still in the Chief's house. He says not everyone will accept Brude, and he is worried the tribe may collapse."

"I do not know about that."

"Who would want to be chief now?" the other girl asked.

Who, indeed? Even Brude, with his monstrous self-confidence, must feel daunted. True made no answer, and the girls put their heads together, whispering and speaking to Tally in soft tones.

Another shadow moved at his side—Barta had returned.

"Is all well?" he asked.

"Nothing is well. So many are hurt both in body and spirit. True, I fear we are lost." Her voice broke on the last word.

Disregarding the girls, True pulled her into his arms. She burrowed in tight, an answer to his ever-present longing.

"Come, Barta. Tally's friends are here to sit with him. Let us step away."

She followed him but a few paces into the deeper darkness. There she moved immediately back into his arms. "Hold me, just hold me," she begged.

He complied, and the moments slipped past in time with their combined heartbeats. He felt her relax almost imperceptibly, and he eased also.

"I have so little to offer them," she breathed into his ear. "Barely even hope."

"There is always hope." He saw an image of himself lying with his throat cut, unable to rise—held from the one place he needed to be, with Barta. "We must pray."

"Yes? And will anyone listen?"

"Oh, yes."

"You think so?"

"I know so."

"Oh, True—what would I do without you? If you weren't with me now, I believe I would sink into darkness, give up, and lay myself down just like Tally."

"No, you would not. You are too strong."

"Just how strong am I, True? Strong enough to sacrifice myself for the good of this tribe? Brude thinks we should wed."

"'We'?" His heart leaped.

"Him—and me. He says it would reassure the tribe, put some of the pieces back together. I believe he really thinks it would lend him legitimacy."

True said nothing.

"Folk would have accepted Wick without question. Brude thinks the promise of my sons—being of Radoc's blood—taking the role in the future will make a difference now." She drew a breath. "But, True, what of you and me?"

He felt the yearning that accompanied the words, and his heart twisted in his chest. A hound understood the need for sacrifice made without question, without hesitation. But he'd already realized he was no longer just a hound. Dared he think about himself?

She stumbled on, the words spouting from her. "I never wanted a husband, never had any time for it. For love. The love I felt for Loyal was enough. Then...then you came into my life."

"Me?" he barely breathed the word.

She tipped up her face as if trying to see his expression in the dark. "If I must wed, I would choose it to be with you. But Brude says the tribe needs the stability of our union—his and mine. And I have been selfish too long. True, what's to be done?"

He had no ready answer to that. In the past he'd

lived moment by moment, knowing only the need to follow at her heels. But he found, as a man, he did not want her to wed with Brude for any reason.

"True, are you willing to wed with me?"

"You know I am willing to give you anything you ask. I will lay down my life for you right now, if you desire it."

"I don't desire that! Anything but that. I want you alive and warm, here in my arms. Brude says if I accept him for husband it would be in appearance only. He would keep Avinda on the side, and I could keep you. But I…I don't think that is good enough for you, True."

"So long as I can remain at your side, it is good enough." Husband, friend, or defender. The decision, he told himself, must be hers, as all the decisions in the past had been. But the thought of Brude having leave to touch her lifted the hairs on the back of his neck.

"If I agree it would be best to wed with him—for the benefit of the tribe—you will not leave me?"

"I will never voluntarily leave you for any reason." If the goddess called an end to this enchantment and forced him away, transformed him back into a dead hound, that would not be his choice. A span of days, she had said but had not declared how many.

"The union with Brude would be for show mostly, but not all," she stumbled on miserably. "There would need to be children, if I wed with him. That—that means…"

True understood very well what it meant, and protest flared more sharply within him. But she'd asked for his reassurance, not his approval.

"If you believe in your heart you must do this thing, I will stand by you. But if you can think of another way, I should be glad."

"I don't know. Tally and I are the last of my father's house. Am I not obligated to serve? And how else can I serve?"

"Tally might take the place of chief."

"He is not ready. And may not be for some time."

Again, True did not speak.

"I promised Brude I would think on it, and that I will do." She reached up and caught his face between her palms. "But if I accept him, if I must make this sacrifice, I want you first. Do you hear me? I will have you first!"

She pressed her mouth to his and her emotions, wild and tumultuous, assailed him. She parted his lips with hers and the flavor of her rushed into him. Completeness found him, so intense he could happily have died there in her arms.

She whimpered, and her tongue swept the inside of his mouth. His body began to shake and he drew her to him—close and closer—to ease his trembling.

Barta broke the kiss long enough to say, "I need you, True, a deep, deep need I barely understand. And I want you. Tell me you want me too."

He did not understand why she would ask him to express desire. Wanting was just wanting, and a hound did not contemplate it. But he desired her the way he wanted his next breath and would withhold from her nothing. "I want you."

"Then we'll make one another a promise: we will lie together as soon as ever we can."

"Here? Now?" Down below, he stood more than ready for it. Her nearness did that to him.

She laughed breathlessly. "With Tally and his

companions so close at hand? Alas, no."

"Then, when?"

She pressed herself still closer and sounded satisfied when she breathed, "Ah, so you are eager for me."

"Yes." He wanted her naked skin against his hide, wanted to taste her as he had before, desired her scent all over him. In an effort to satisfy himself he claimed her mouth, licked the inside of it deeply, and grew still harder below.

She slid her arms around his neck but broke the kiss to say, "So it is promised. Whether I accept Brude or no—and I have not decided that yet—I will have you first inside me."

He struggled to clear his mind amid the sweet fog of desire. "Yet if we mate, might you not then go to him already bred by me? What then?"

"Then the chief's hut will still hold the seed of the last chief—and the truest Caledonii warrior I have ever known."

Chapter Twenty-Two

Respite, at last. Weariness, bone deep, warred inside Barta with the desire for True that had ridden her for days while the tribe moved ever eastward toting wounded, distressed children, and a dismayingly small number of belongings. Now at last Brude had called a halt on the banks of a stream and begun setting up a rough camp. A collective sigh of relief—felt more than heard—migrated through the tribe.

The rear guard insisted they had not been followed. Gant himself had told Barta so when she questioned him, having been one of the men sweeping their trail. Barta wondered if she dared relax and catch her breath, take time to regain her strength. And, perhaps, at last lie with True?

She set down her burdens—two packs and a number of weapons—and eyed him as he busied himself getting Tally settled. Her young brother, now on his feet, was unable to match the pace Brude had set, and True had helped him most of the way. Tally, a boy always in motion, found his continued limitations as hard to bear as his grief, and Barta worried for him. He seemed sunk into the same gloom she occupied.

More than once had she heard him weeping in the night. But then, the sound of quiet weeping had become commonplace among members of the tribe once the sun went down.

At least Tally had his own followers—the group of girls who accompanied him had increased to four in number; Barta rarely had a chance to do much for him. The girls served to distract him from his thoughts and perhaps provided some comfort, even as True lent her.

True...she derived such pleasure just in watching him, the grace and economy of his movements, the beauty of his narrow face and the way it brightened impossibly when he smiled at Tally. She allowed her gaze to caress his shaggy hair, like a wild mane down his back, and admire the supple body beneath the shabby clothes he wore. The very prospect of that body pressed against her own brought the heat up into her face and stole her breath away.

Tonight? Perhaps, but there was so much to do first. Arrange for shelter, check the state of the wounded, fetch water and provide food for all. And she still owed an answer to Brude. Twice had he come to her looking for acceptance of his proposal of marriage—something to lend the tribe heart, as he put it. Both times had she put him off, but she knew all too well he would soon be at her elbow again.

True looked up and caught her gaze upon him. His eyes brightened and greater heat kindled between them, this time touching her heart. Oh, by the sweet goddess, how she loved him! She needed to tell him so over again, show him with every part of her body and her being, bond with him beyond the reach of Brude and the rest of the world.

If there was one comfort left to her, one thing that made her grasp hold of life and hold on, it was True...

"Barta?"

She gasped, the magical spell woven between

herself and True trembling like the threads of a spider's web, but not breaking. She turned to find Brude beside her. Indeed, that had not taken him long.

But Brude looked a man changed—as weary, filthy, and worried as she, his hair hanging in a tangle and his eyes hollow. She felt an unexpected twinge of sympathy.

He nodded toward Tally and his group of attendants. "How fares he?"

Barta could not but wonder why he asked—out of concern, was it, or did he imagine a fully recovered Tally might make a threat to his place as chief? And, she chided herself, who would want the place? Only look what it made of the dauntless Brude!

She shrugged and grimaced. "Improving, but he has no endurance yet. It might be better were we to stay in one place more than a night."

"We shall be staying here for the time being. We'll take time to tend our sick and wounded and make a few decisions. I think if the Gaels intended to pursue us, we would know of it by now. Our men have seen nothing yet."

"Good." But Barta felt uneasy down to her bones. She glanced about. "Brude, do you not think it strange we have come all this way yet have met with the members of no other tribe? We should be on Chief Cunobar's land by now. Why have we encountered none of his guard?"

"That worries me also. He was a good ally to your father. Quite frankly, that is one of the reasons I moved us east. I hoped to speak with him of joining forces."

"What do you think it means?"

Brude shook his head. "Perhaps he has also shifted

his folk farther east, or north. We may yet meet up with them. For now, we will build a camp here."

"That is well."

He glanced aside to where True now assisted Pith to sit as comfortably as possible. The old man, his hut having been situated apart from the main settlement, had not lost his possessions to fire and insisted on bringing a large number of them along. True had carried most of those belongings all this day.

Barta assumed Brude assessed the old man's condition, but when he spoke his words did not concern Pith.

"Barta, have you made up your mind?"

She caught her breath. "Not yet."

Brude turned his hollow eyes on her. "You need to make your choice soon. We have to put the pieces of the tribe back together, for their sake. This would be a good place for that."

Even though Barta had expected this—and set herself for it—panic licked up through her now. She shook her head.

Brude snapped. "Still entirely selfish, are you? I was hoping you had changed, but it seems you can think of nothing but your own desires. Have you never heard of sacrifice?"

"I've been instructed in it by the best." The very best.

"Then it is time for you to embrace that teaching. This is survival. Think how ashamed of you your father would be."

Barta stood motionless, unable to speak for her hurt.

True, still at a distance, turned his head in Barta's

direction as if he felt her flare of distress. Certainly he couldn't hear Brude's words, not unless he had the hearing of a hound.

Around the lump of pain in her throat she choked out, "I am surprised you would consider taking me for wife when you still hold so harsh an opinion of me."

"I have no choice. I can think only of the welfare of the tribe—as must you. I will have your answer in the morning, understand?"

Not awaiting a reply, he stalked away, leaving Barta drenched with cold.

****

"What did Master Brude say to you? He upset you, so I could tell."

Deep darkness had fallen once again. Here on the banks of the quiet stream a few fires burned low—Barta could just glimpse the nearest, tended by Tally's friends. The girls had made him supper and stayed with him while he ate it.

Exhausted, many members of the tribe already slept. Not far away, Pith had rolled into his blankets; across the camp Brude and Avinda sat with their heads close together. Children had been tucked among rugs, and a measure of peace spread slowly through the trees.

Barta, who ached with weariness, had expected True's question but felt nearly incapable of answering it. She snuggled closer to his side, and his arm snaked about her; the breath came easier in her lungs.

All she wanted was the peace and pleasure of his company, without discord. She sighed. "He asked once again for my answer. He says he will have it come morning."

True said nothing but, this close to him, she could

feel the protest jerk through his body.

"He insists our union will stabilize the tribe. And I do want that, I want to put our pieces back together if I can. If I have, in fact, left my selfishness behind me, should I not accept him?"

"You ask me?" True's rough voice sounded like a growl.

"Should I not? Speaking with you feels almost like talking to myself."

"You would do better talking to Gant. He understands these matters far better than me."

"What matters?"

"Of the heart, of the choices people make for themselves and one another."

"Perhaps he does understand those things, but I am not in love with Gant."

For an instant neither of them breathed, but the connection between them flared and demanded acknowledgement.

At last he whispered, "I have told you I will be with you no matter the choice you make."

"With me, yes, but in what way?"

"At your side. Fighting for you, always at your call."

"I want you in my bed, True. You—not him. I thought you understood that."

"Me first, so you said. Before you accept him. Yet you will accept him."

"I may have no choice. It is not what I want. But it has been brought upon me—I believe the goddess works to impress upon me—that sacrifices must sometimes be made."

"So they must." In the dim light, she saw him close

his eyes like a man in pain. "Barta, if you must go to his bed, it will not change the way I feel about you."

"Nothing can?"

"Nothing can," he agreed.

"But does that not make it all the more wrong that I should go to his bed, when you and I are so closely bound? It should be you, only you." At the urging of instinct she pressed her mouth to his, lips parted, wooing him into her. She could not get close enough, not unless he became part of her and they one.

He tasted the inside of her mouth with long, slow sweeps of his tongue that banished every other thought, every worry, and turned her blood molten. Her heart began to pound in demand.

When he turned his attentions to her cheek and her throat, moving downward in a blaze of heat, she said, "I want you tonight, True. Before I give him my answer. I will have you."

He said nothing, merely drew her down to lie beneath him on the ground. His fingers threaded through the laces at her bosom and teased them apart. She felt his tongue at her breast.

But she seized his head in both hands. "Do you hear me, True? Do you understand?"

"You wish to give yourself to me."

"Completely."

"Completely."

"Then we will always have this even if…well, whatever else happens. This will remain sacred between us. Do you agree?"

"I exist only for you, in any way you ask."

"But…" She strove once more to see the expression in his eyes. "Do you want me also?"

"Do I want you? Only as I want my next breath, as I want my heart to keep beating. No, even more than those things."

A gust of breath left her lungs, a sigh that contained both gladness and longing. "Need," she whispered.

"Yes. I need to taste you, every part of you. Need to feel in full these bonds between us."

"Then show me."

"What of the guard? Should they stumble upon us…"

"They will not, here. If they should, let them. I mean to have you this night."

He began tugging at her clothing, spending no more words. She shed her garments eagerly and without shame, more sure of this than anything that had ever come before. She pulled at his clothing also, her hands shaking with need.

When they were both naked, when their bodies met skin on skin in the soft dark, it felt so wonderful she gasped.

"Kiss me," she begged and their mouths met, their bodies met, and she felt him in full.

Let me have this if but once, she begged the goddess, and I will never ask for another thing.

True broke their kiss, licked her lips, and dragged his tongue down her body, past her throat, her breasts, and lower still. She felt his teeth nip very gently at the skin of her belly before he lifted her effortlessly beneath him, the muscles of his stomach flexing. Not until he started to flip her over did she gasp again.

"True? What—"

He set her on her elbows and knees and positioned

himself behind her, nipped her shoulder and licked it in consolation.

"What are you doing?" she asked.

"Mating you."

A wild, delirious laugh rose to Barta's throat. "But, like this?"

"Certainly. How else?"

Barta's mind lashed madly. Was this how men and women made love in the north? Arousing, without a doubt, but—

"I was hoping this time—our first time—we might join face to face."

"Eh?"

"As people do."

"People?"

Laughter bubbled up again. "People such as us. We are not animals."

He froze for an instant; she could feel his thoughts racing. He breathed, "You must show me."

"Well, I have never…"

"Nor have I, not with any woman."

"Oh?"

"But I wish to join with you in this way, Barta."

She flipped back over beneath him and drew a ragged breath, all her laughter flown. "Then listen to your body. Follow as it bids."

He nodded, joined his mouth to hers, and began to move. She wound her arms around his neck and followed.

There would be pain the first time, she knew that much. At this moment she didn't care. She felt alive for him, aware and sensitized. Her love for him rose in a staggering wave, lit by fire.

She dug her fingers into his hair and wooed him with her body. He nudged her thighs apart and—just as easily as breathing, as being—slid inside her, a knife coming home to its sheath where it belonged. No pain, only the shattering sense of rightness, and completeness that defied description. They moved together to an ancient rhythm, fully joined, and hung like a star in the sky before they came as one.

Perfection, full and exquisite. Barta scarcely dared breathe for breaking the spell. True remained inside her, close as flesh could be to flesh, their mouths still fused. Emotion barreled through her and tears pricked her eyes.

Now nothing would be the same for either of them, not ever again.

Chapter Twenty-Three

All thought had emptied from True's mind, drained away in the wake of the passion. Only belonging remained, that which he'd sought every instant since returning to Barta—this sense of wholeness, of peace.

Who knew it might be like this, that two could become one flesh, creating a being so much more than either alone? Part of him still remained inside her. The miracle of that stunned him; he didn't want to withdraw from her and cause this wondrous moment to end.

Eyes closed in fierce bliss, he licked the inside of her mouth slowly. The scent of her filled him, the taste had become part of him. He needed nothing more.

She made a small sound in the back of her throat and stroked his tongue with hers. No words were needed now. He'd already emptied his seed inside her but could feel himself growing ready to do so again.

Barta had been right—face to face, heart to heart, was much better, and one flesh best of all.

And oh, how they fit together! He flexed his hips, demonstrating to her his return to readiness, and she moaned, still while sucking on his tongue.

Receptive, yes. Fire roared through him, surpassing anything he'd ever felt as a hound.

She quickened, her inner muscles once more tensing around him. By the goddess, what a marvelous sensation! As if to some music of the gods, they began to move once more in a primal dance.

Barta loosened her grip on his hair, trailed her fingers down his back, caressing his muscles as she went, and cupped his naked buttocks. She broke the kiss to say, "Need you. Like this, just like this."

Still devoid of words, he bunched his shoulders and dove for her breast. She arched beneath him, and her muscles began to milk him from within.

"Oh, wondrous," she gasped in his ear when he emptied himself again. "Wondrous."

Still unwilling to separate from her, he collapsed with his mouth beside her ear, his heart racing. "You," he breathed, "are now well and truly bred."

"I am, aren't I? And glad of it."

"Are you glad?"

"Yes."

"Even if I have given you my…child?"

"I am glad!"

As was he. But he wondered what the goddess would make of it. This hadn't been part of his bargain with her. He'd asked only to return to Barta, not breed her, and he could scarcely imagine such a child.

A gentle breeze stirred, drying the sweat on his back. Barta whispered, "If you want to do it the other way—from behind—I'm willing." She rubbed her cheek against his. "I am willing to do anything you ask."

"I am satisfied." He made as if to withdraw from her; she clasped her palms more tightly on his buttocks, preventing him.

"No. Stay."

Ah, a command he understood. He eased and ran his tongue along her shoulder, gathering the salt.

She laughed softly. "If you do that, I shall need you again."

"Still. You need me still."

"Yes."

So she felt it too, this profound sense of joining... What could one do with such a gift but accept it? He licked her again, a slow, leisurely swipe of his tongue. "By the goddess, you taste good. As good as you smell. I want to taste you everywhere."

"I want what you want. Have I not said so? Go ahead."

"Are you certain?"

"I belong to you now, True."

"No, it is I who belong to you—I always have."

"We belong to one another, sure and strong. Can you feel the bonds?"

"Yes."

"Unbreakable."

That, he understood. Had he not returned to her from death because their ties endured?

"And so, True, I give my body to you along with my heart. Do as you will with it."

"I will protect you always. Cherish you. Die in your defense if I must."

She froze, suddenly rigid. "Why do you keep saying that? It is the last thing I want. I've already experienced the loss of so many beloved and could not endure it again...could not bear losing you! That is why I am glad I've had you this night, even if we are never to be together again."

His heart fell. "Do you say we will not?"

"I have not decided what I should tell Brude, have I?"

True did not want her to wed with Brude, did not want any other male to touch her, ever. But it was not his place to make demands. It was his place to follow and accept what she offered him. And this night she offered herself completely.

Very gently he withdrew from her. She murmured in protest.

"But, Mistress, you have given me leave to taste you. Everywhere."

"Oh. Even—?"

"Where we were joined." The scent coming from there he found most arousing of all.

She sighed in complete submission. "Do as you will."

****

"I need your answer, Barta. The tribe must regain stability. We have to make plans."

Barta stood before Brude in the morning sunshine—a woman changed. Some fundamental need inside her had been answered and at the same time awakened. She could not think about True without desiring him and could not seem to think of anything but him. Even now, away from him for the first time since the long, deep night, her senses tracked him and the bonds between them hummed.

She regarded Brude with new calm. A man with a great heavy burden on his shoulders, she no longer wanted to battle him.

She looked him in the eye. "Something you should know before you hear my answer—I am in love with True."

He grimaced. "You think that is a surprise to me? I've seen the way you look at one another. I do not care.

Haven't I said you are welcome to keep him on the side?"

"Yes." She jerked her head up a notch. "But I tell you now fairly, he and I did lie together. I may be carrying his child."

Rage blossomed in Brude's eyes, a blazing wall of disparagement. He raised his arm, and for an instant Barta believed he would strike her down.

"Foolish girl! Stupid, selfish girl. Could you not control your impulses? I thought you said you'd learned something from all our losses!"

People around them stared; Brude had raised his voice along with his hand. From the corner of her eye Barta saw True materialize and approach.

I will protect you always. Cherish you. Die in your defense if I must.

Would Brude turn upon True if he tried to defend her? He seemed angry enough.

She took a careful step backward and asked, "Do you still want me for wife, in this condition?"

Brude's face worked for a moment, his eyes glinting dangerously. "Did I not tell you to have a care over that?"

"You did—once we wed. We are not yet wed, and my body is mine to give as I will."

"You understood my meaning and have deliberately defied me. You have not changed— perhaps you never will. You deserve a thrashing."

"Barta?" True stepped into place at her side. He touched her arm lightly, and strength flooded through her.

"It's all right, True."

" 'True,' " Brude sneered once again. "What a lie

of a name. He might be anything but that—any type of snake sent to suckle at our bosom."

"I trust him completely."

"More fool you. I do not trust him." He intensified his glare at True. "Just so you know, incomer, there will come a reckoning between us."

True spoke softly, yet with that ever-present growl in his voice, "There is no sense in us fighting one another when enemies lie all around."

"Yes, and perhaps within." Brude switched his glare back to Barta. "You did this just to defy me, did you not?"

"No." Barta tangled her fingers with True's. "I have told you why. He and I belong together…"

Brude virtually spat, "Well, he can have you. You are of no use to me bred by another. Stupid woman! Could you not make one sacrifice for your tribe?"

"I will make many sacrifices. Not that one."

"Get out of my sight," Brude barked, sounding uncannily like Radoc the night Barta had come home to admit she'd lost Loyal.

Was she truly the selfish wretch Brude insisted? Did she still think only of herself? But her heart had changed.

True tugged her fingers, and she turned away, only then noticing a small crowd had gathered around them. Folk, already shattered, stared. Had they all heard? Did they even now make judgments of her?

She caught a glimpse of Gant, his expression tight, and one of the girls who'd been tending Tally. She didn't want word of this getting back to her young brother, who'd always looked up to her and so often taken her part.

Despair touched her heart. She followed True to the stream in silence and moved into his arms.

"True, am I the terrible person Brude accuses?"

"No." True's hands cradled her. She felt his lips brush her hair, weaving a spell which she tried to shrug off. She needed clarity now, if ever. Had her parents overindulged her? Given her a life of privilege? Her mother had certainly lectured and her father berated her often enough. Sudden longing filled her for her mother's wisdom and her father's strong guidance.

Gone now—swept away with her past life. Wick had left; she had only Tally, Gant, and this man in her arms.

She lifted her head from his shoulder and gazed into his eyes. That same wave of familiarity—for someone she could not quite place—swept over her, silent recognition so profound it left her on the very edge of realization.

"Who are you?" she breathed. "Who—?"

His lips parted. Before he could speak, someone came running; one of the girls who had been tending Tally called Barta's name. Barta turned to see Tally struggling along in the girl's wake, leaning on the arm of yet another girl. Tally, face pale, wore a determined look that aged him beyond his years.

Barta stood quietly until he reached them, her hand still resting on True's arm. Why had she never before noticed how very much Tally looked like their mother? Her heart twisted in her breast.

"Tally, you should not be moving about so much."

Grimly, he met her gaze. "It seems I must." He jerked his head toward the encampment. "I heard about what happened back there." The strength of iron appeared in his gray eyes. "Sister, it is time I was up on my feet. And it is time you and I together took back this tribe—on Wick's behalf, and on Father's."

Chapter Twenty-Four

"I know who you are." Tally spoke quietly as they sat beside the fire, his words meant for True's ears alone. Unemphatic as they were, they set True's every instinct on alert.

He looked at the boy sharply. Tally sat with a rug slung over his shoulders against the cold and damp, his hair hanging in a tangle. Like the rest of them, he looked weary and miserable, but strength kindled in his eyes. They met True's head-on, and a chill traced its way up True's spine.

Another day had passed, a time of confusion and unrest among the members of the Epidii. For the moment, he and the lad sat alone; Barta had gone to speak with Gant and others of the guard, and Tally's friends were off on some errand for him. Now True wondered if Tally had sent them just so he might have this opportunity to speak privately.

True shrugged uncomfortably and looked away from those perceptive eyes. "I do not understand your meaning, young Master. How could you know what no one else does? I barely remember my own past."

Tally's lips curved in a wry smile. "Oh, you remember it. Why else would you call me 'young Master' when none of us here are your masters? You are a poor liar...True. So you should be, with such a name."

True swallowed convulsively as heat suffused him. He had not been prepared for this; since yesterday he'd thought about little but Barta and Brude, and what the breakdown in relations between them might mean for the tribe. He'd questioned himself over and over again, because if the goddess decided to recall him into death—his miraculous time here suddenly done—he would have to leave Barta in perilous circumstances indeed.

Now he wondered how best to reply to Tally. Prevarication seemed hopeless, denial useless.

Before he could speak, Tally went on very softly, "I think my mother knew also, did she not, or at least suspected? It is why she defended you from the moment you returned. She had an instinct for all things magical, did Mother. I suppose I've inherited a bit of that."

True drew a breath that seared his lungs. "Young Master…Barta does not know. She cannot be told or the spell ends. Should she guess, I have leave from the goddess to tell her, but anything else will sunder us. You cannot breathe a word."

"You think I would?" Again, Tally's smoky gray gaze engaged True's and held it. "Indeed, I am surprised Barta has not yet guessed. Your eyes are the same—exactly the same. By what miracle did you win your way back to us?"

"By the mercy of the Lady, her reward for the loyalty I'd shown." True shook his head. "But it is not forever, and she would not say how long I might stay. I didn't care, at the beginning. I wanted only to arise and follow your sister—in any form."

Compassion flooded Tally's gaze. "I saw her

agony when she lost you. I had never seen anyone hurt that way. I confess, I never thought on your pain at being unable to take the place at her side as always. Are you sure Barta does not guess?"

"I am sure."

"Yet I have never known her to take to anyone as readily as she did to you. My sister is not what I would describe as a warm woman and not particularly welcoming to strangers. Yet she did welcome you at once. And she must feel something strong—else she'd never have taken you to her bed."

True stared. "What do you know of that?"

"Rekka told me. She overheard what Barta said to Brude. Is it the truth, or just a lie Barta told to put Brude off?"

"It's the truth." True closed his eyes for an instant, remembering the perfection of those moments when he and Barta became one—and he became complete. They had not joined so since, though she did lie beside him when she slept.

True did not know what to do with the feelings that filled him when he looked at her or recalled her touch, the sweet taste of her. It made a powerful hunger. And now he faced this danger, if Tally could be considered a danger.

"Please, young Master," he whispered, his eyes still squeezed shut—a prayer. "Do not tell her."

For an instant Tally remained silent. Then True felt the boy's fingers grip his forearm hard. "Do you think I would betray you, True?" he asked again. "That I would betray the goddess, for all that, at whose feet I worship? That I would destroy this finely woven spell of magic it is my privilege to witness? What do you say happens if Barta does guess who you really are?"

True looked at him then, his heart in his eyes. "My understanding is I will then win leave to stay."

Tally nodded his head, looking thoughtful. "It can only be a matter of time before she sees the spirit that inhabits this flesh—the same spirit, as I can clearly perceive, she's loved so long. I will keep your secret, True. In the meantime, I would like to think of you as an ally."

True regarded Tally curiously, and the boy went on, "I do not completely understand why Wick left. He must have known it would be the last thing our parents would wish. Father wanted one of his children to take the place of chief after him. With Wick gone, that leaves Barta. Or me."

True lowered his voice still further. "I do not know that your sister wants the place." He looked away across the encampment to where he could just glimpse Barta in conversation with Gede.

"Are you quite certain? For I believe she always longed to lead, deep down. It is why she defied Father so often, and it's what prompted the raid that cost her so very much."

"Perhaps loss has changed her mind."

"But we need someone to step up now. Master True, I remember little of the attack at my parents' hut, when they were killed. But while I lay senseless after, I had dreams. Deep, surprising dreams."

"Did you?" True sometimes dreamed of running as a hound, his paws flying over the rough ground and the air rushing through his lungs.

"I dreamed of us all together the way it used to be before Father got injured so sorely."

197

"And why was that surprising?"

Tally smiled. "Only because I could feel the magic that surrounded us all, uniting us—like love. Mother used to say there was magic in everything—that it bound the world together, if we could but see."

"Yes."

"It's as if in this dream state I could see the love—and magic—underlying everything, making of us a tribe. But what it united was not flesh with flesh so much as spirit with spirit."

True looked at the boy questioningly.

"What I am saying to you," Tally told him softly, "is that the bond never breaks and love never ends. We are all still united, and that means I must act in my Father's stead, if Barta will not."

"You?"

"I know I am young. But I have strong friends around me—Gede, Gant, my sister...and you."

"You mean to challenge Brude for the place?" True asked carefully.

"Why not? My sister has no issue, yet. And that makes me the last surviving member of my father's house. I have almost fifteen winters. And I am willing."

"You would make a fine leader, Master Tally, were you older. You have wisdom and, as you say, a share of your mother's magic. But in such times as these, with unrest all around, the Gaels on our heels, and winter coming...would Brude make such a poor leader? He has strength and a desire for it."

"But little compassion and limited wisdom. I dread to think what mistakes he might make."

Gently, True said, "Young Master, we all make mistakes. Brude, Barta, me."

"And I will make them also. But they will not be mistakes prompted by arrogance or greed. And I will not let us forget our spiritual duties, what we owe the Lord and Lady. You, above all, should acknowledge that."

True bowed his head.

Tally went on slowly, "I pray the Gaels will pursue us no farther this season. They have what they want for now—the land we held." Tally's wide gaze grew hazy, as if he looked inward. True recalled sometimes seeing such a mist in Mistress Essa's eyes. Softly, Tally spoke. "Yes, they have what they want for now. But it will not last. They will send their clans in the wake of their war carts; they will spread all across the land that once belonged to the Caledonii, like a sickness. In my dreams I have Seen a time when our language is lost and even our blood is but a memory in this land."

True went breathless. "How to fight such a thing? If you have Seen—"

"What I have Seen is a warning. I believe it will take might and magic together if we are to stay free. Brude's path will bring ruination." Tally gripped True's arm. "I have told no one else of this, nor can you. I will keep your secret if you keep mine."

True did not like keeping secrets, and the one he already guarded weighed heavily enough. But the boy's aura had altered and changed color to something resembling that of Mistress Essa's.

He nodded reluctantly, and Tally's fingers tightened. "Good. Now come along with me. There is much to be done."

Chapter Twenty-Five

"You?" Brude's stern face broke into sudden laughter, unexpected and cruel as a bolt of lightning. He shot an incredulous look at True before returning his stare to Tally, who stood before him straight as a sapling.

True concentrated on making his own expression blank, revealing none of his thoughts. Tally had insisted on going to Brude at once and stating his case. They hadn't even taken the matter to Barta first.

"Oh, Tally, boy, thank you for the laugh. I thought I might never laugh so again."

"Scoff if you will; I am in earnest."

"You cannot possibly be. Look at you! How many years have you now?"

"Almost fifteen."

"Fifteen years. And you think you can take Wick's place?"

"No, my father's place."

Brude gave another disdainful bark of laughter. "Go away, boy. I have work to do."

Tally jerked his chin up a notch. "Flight, you mean? The ceding of our lands—presenting them to the Gaels like a gift? Just," he added deliberately, "what you chided my father for doing."

All humor drained from Brude's face. "I have presented them with nothing," he stated. "I have merely moved eastward in an effort to save all these lives." He waved an arm to encompass the camp at large. "We have too few warriors, especially given your sister's rashness and your brother's defection. How am I to make a stand with no men?"

"There comes a time when one must stand no matter the numbers. That was hallowed ground we gave up, where lay the bones of our ancestors."

Tally's voice had risen, shrill with his youth. Folk began to drift up; True felt more than saw Barta glance their way.

"So," Brude hunched his shoulders and took it on, "you would drench it with still more Epidii blood? All this land is hallowed ground. Without more warriors, we will not hold any of it."

"What goes on here?" Barta, breathless, took the place at True's side.

Brude snapped, "What goes on is that your cub of a brother fancies himself a wolf full grown. He thinks to challenge me."

Barta stared, and a muscle bunched in Tally's jaw. "Someone must."

"Tally"—Barta laid a hand on the boy's arm— "come away. This is but the pain in your heart speaking." She looked at True. "Why did you let him speak?"

"It is not my place to hold him."

That caused Brude to direct a glare at True. "And you would not, if you could. I have noticed, True"—he made a curse of the name—"whenever trouble erupts, you are to be found nearby. I do not care how many trials you have overcome." He raised his voice and spoke to those still drifting up, one of whom was Gant.

"Does anyone else worry about the danger he represents?"

Gant spoke up, after a measured glance at True. "He has fought bravely in every encounter we've shared."

"So he has. But that could be a ruse. He might well be a spy."

Barta pushed past Tally and stood nose to nose with Brude. "This has little to do with True. You merely seek to divert blame from what you have done in seizing the place of chief."

"Blame? It is not I responsible for the death of brave warriors whose strong arms we now need so desperately. And not I who took this dangerous incomer to her bed!"

A murmur circulated through the onlookers.

Tally spoke before Barta could. "He is not dangerous. I have Seen!"

"Ah, now you would claim your mother's place as well as your father's?"

"I claim only what the gods have granted me."

True closed his eyes a moment, hoping Tally in his earnestness would not spill his secret.

He felt Barta's fingers brush his arm before she said, "It does not matter whom I take to my bed."

"That is where you are wrong." Brude's expression turned ugly. "Your sons will have a place in the succession." Wildly, he gestured at True. "Do we want them descended from that?"

Once again, the crowd murmured. True felt a chill work its way up his spine. Could his presence ultimately harm Barta? As a hound, his presence at her side had not mattered. As a person, he may already have given her his child, quite possibly the next Chief of the Epidii.

Again, Tally spoke up. "The past—and those gone before us—are with us yet, so long as I stand. Those who would support me as chief, rally round. Those who would have Brude lead us, do likewise to him. We shall let the gods decide which of us should lead the Epidii."

The murmur among the onlookers rose to a clamor. For an instant True's ears, overwhelmed, could distinguish few distinct words.

Brude threw back his head. "Finish growing up, boy, before you think to challenge me. Perhaps it is time for a new order. Given your sister's foolishness, your brother's defection, and your own childishness, what has Radoc's house to offer us now?"

Out of the ensuing furor stepped Pith. Respected the old man was, despite his blindness. Some argued he had a direct connection with the powers, and few would doubt it now when he lifted his face to the sky and to each of those at the forefront in turn, precisely as if he could see them.

"Brude map Edder," he began, "you take much upon yourself. You have snatched this place as chief with none to grant it to you and think to hold it now in defiance of our traditions. What did Radoc map Dumno ever do but fight on our behalf? Since the time of his uncle and his grandfather before him, those of his blood have spent themselves for our sakes." The old man's voice quavered a bit before he resumed yet more strongly, "I remember his grandfather, knew him in my youth. He would despise us for running now. Yet it is the first course you, self-appointed chief, chose."

Brude rounded on him, little respect for the elder's

position visible on his face. "I am no coward. Indeed, I did argue to Radoc in the past that we should fight. It is my first course of action. But I moved as I did to preserve what is left of this tribe—to buy us more time and give us a chance to recover. You shall not label me 'coward'!"

Quickly Tally spoke, his voice piping high above the others but his words unflinching. "I say we should go back, take up our old stance, and fight for what belongs to us." He raised his chin still higher. "Either way, I say leadership of this tribe should not be handed over to Brude while members of our house still stand!"

****

"Sister, we need to work together. It's the only thing that will serve."

Barta shot Tally a look and marveled again at the change in him. A different being from the grief-stricken and injured boy he'd been only days ago, he now appeared fired with a determination that lit him from within. Transformed he was, and no mistake.

She could recall her mother wearing just that look when spiritually convinced about some course of action. Was it possible Tally had inherited the best of both their parents?

Lifting a brow, she considered it. The two of them sat alone beside their fire in the dull afternoon, overcast and chilly enough to herald winter.

Barta could not bear thinking of winter with its want and hardships—not now. How dared Tally look so confident?

"Do we not always work together?" she asked, quoting one of Essa's favorite adages. "It is the path to survival."

Tally turned his misty gray eyes on her. "You know very well what I mean. Despite what Brude says, you are not stupid." A small smile curled his lips. "Well, not usually."

Barta sighed. She wished True would return from tending the injured hounds, many now without masters and bearing sore wounds. They responded well to True, and he'd gathered them on the far side of the camp.

Important work, but she never felt at ease without him at her side—just as she could no longer seem to sleep except in his arms.

Last night while there she'd dreamed she slept with Loyal instead, his scent surrounding her. For an instant after she woke she'd been sure it was so: not till her eyes caught sight of True's fingers splayed across her breast had the pieces fallen back into place. Troubling and yet strangely comforting at the same time. But she needed his presence—like breath.

A bit tartly she told Tally, "I understand you are bent on taking Wick's place. That does not mean you need to take up with insulting me."

"I do not insult you. Nor do I mean to take Wick's place. I mean to make a new place for myself—and you. We are the only ones left, Barta. We must rise to it and stand together."

"A boy of fifteen and a woman who's lost whatever respect she ever garnered from this tribe?"

"Radoc's descendants."

"Against Brude with all his strengths, and given the fact that, with Wick gone, most of the young warriors will seek to follow him."

"Most—not all. We have strengths also, and we do not stand alone. Old loyalties die hard. We have Gant on our side and, I believe, Gede as well. Gartnait, Pith…and True."

"Pith? He is old, Tally, and blind."

"You heard him speak up for us. And he possesses a great deal of wisdom; folk will listen to him. He also approves of True."

Yes, Barta acknowledged ruefully—one of the few who did. "All well and good," she told Tally, "but do you not see? Ranging up those who will and will not support us may well serve to split the tribe. We are already weak enough."

"I do not believe it will sunder us. We are at a point of decision, yes. Do we continue to run, or do we go back and reclaim the land where our ancestors lie?"

"Tally"—Barta reached out and touched his hand—"I admire your spirit, I do. For all your youth you shame me with your courage and determination to fight. But we are not the tribe we were. It might be best to wait for spring before staging any acts of defiance."

"By spring the Gaels will be well dug in. They will have time to bring in more of their folk—more weapons and more accursed chariots. I say hit them now while they—just like we—have suffered some losses. Did you not say they suffered casualties in that raid you led?"

"Yes."

"And still more in the attack upon our settlement. I do not say we should stage battle proper against them. But a series of raids could hurt them."

"That is what I thought." Barta swallowed hard. "Only look what it cost."

"Sister, you have lost your confidence. How will you get it back again? You were never so humble and biddable, and I cannot imagine you at Brude's heel."

Neither could Barta. But she said, "My selfishness has been well pointed out to me over and over again. It is past time I grew up."

"You are right that this is no time for selfishness." Unexpectedly Tally grinned. "If it were, I'd just enjoy Rekka's company and that of the other girls who quite suddenly flock around me, thinking I may one day become chief.

"But, Sister, there is selfishness and there is strength. Those of our line have long been chiefs for good reason; we do not give up easily. Did Father give up when he suffered his terrible injury?"

"No." Indeed, only slaughter had put an end to that bright courage. "But what of Wick, whose heart and spine were not up to the task set before him?"

Tally's eyes gazed inward for an instant and turned misty. "My brother is no coward and will return. It's up to us to hold things together until he does."

"I must say I would not mind seeing Brude put in his place. But, Tally, I fear I have lost too much…"

"You have also gained much. Ah, here he comes now." Tally slanted a look at her. "Your courage. To be sure, he never stays long away from you."

Barta jerked her head around and saw True approaching, his gaze fixed upon her. At once some yearning inside her eased; she drew a deep breath.

"There, now." A note of puzzlement entered Tally's voice. "And does he not remind you of someone, Sister?"

"Yes, very much." Barta let her gaze range over the man who came at a graceful lope, his shaggy hair gleaming in the weak afternoon sun. "But I will be accursed if I can put my finger on it."

"You had best try, if you mean to make him the father of your children." Tally lowered his voice as True reached them. "You would not want him to slip away from you."

"No," Barta agreed. "Never."

Chapter Twenty-Six

"So what do you think of our Tally?" Barta breathed the question into True's ear when all had become still later that night.

He'd just finished filling her with his seed, arching his body in a movement so strong and beautiful it stole all words—all thought, for that matter. But now the sense of completeness that always found her when they were together and so closely bound allowed her to find her strength and her voice.

Nearly a fortnight had passed since her conversation with her brother. He'd spent the time moving about the tribe, speaking with everyone and employing a combination of their father's determination and their mother's charm. Testing the waters, Tally called it, when she asked him.

Brude watched it all from a distance and with a scowl. He did not interfere with Tally's movements but continued to give the day-to-day orders that kept the tribe safe—chose and assigned the guard, set the squads for hut raising and firewood gathering.

At least he no longer came around Barta—lying with True had put paid to that, just as it had answered the deepest need of her soul.

She ran her palms down his naked back and drew him closer, though in truth it would be impossible for them to get much closer.

Before answering her question, he licked her cheek—an odd habit, though True did seem to favor it and she had no objections. She parted her lips for him, and their mouths fused again in a long and searing kiss.

She moved her hands into his hair and felt heat spread through her body again.

When at last the kiss ended, she murmured, "I thought we were done."

"I will never be done with you. Never have enough."

Her heart convulsed in her chest. "I do not know what miracle brought you to me. I am half afraid to question it. Mother used to say believing in things makes them so. And, True, what can I do but believe? When we are together like this I feel complete inside, every need answered."

He went still. "Yet you still want to know how it is I came to you—and from whence."

Could he read her mind as well as sense her every desire?

"It is just that folk have been coming to me and asking. Word has got round, you see, that we are lying together. And my sons will be in line for the succession. Folk would like to be certain about the man who will father those sons."

He slid his fingers down from her breast to her belly in a gentle caress. "Do you think you are carrying my child?"

"I don't know, do I?" The frequency and vigor with which he loved her argued it could only be a matter of time. And her heart leaped to embrace the possibility, one of purest joy.

Even if she brought a child forth into an uncertain

world of battle and strife, it would be his child.

She felt him draw a breath. "Mayhap it would be best, Mistress, if I do not breed you again."

Barta stiffened in protest. "Why should you say such a thing?"

He took a moment before he answered, motionless in her arms. "The magic that brought me to you will not last forever. I might be called away at any time without warning."

"No."

"Mayhap I should have reminded myself—and you—of that before ever we lay together, before we kissed. For now, Mistress, the ties between us feel so strong and so tight, I do not understand how I ever can leave you."

"You cannot. You will not! Do you hear me?" Barta tried to imagine a future without him, a deep and wrenching loss beyond expressing.

"And," she went on before he could answer, "do not call me that. Why have you begun with calling me 'Mistress' once again? I thought you'd decided to call me—"

"Barta." He spoke it into her ear, and she felt magic swirl all around them, battling her terror. "I have no wish to leave you ever. Being with you is the one desire of my heart. But I felt you should remember, should I give you a child, I may not have leave to stay and help you raise it. So make your choice now when there is a chance you are not yet carrying—and I will not lie with you again."

Tears stung Barta's eyes; she fought them back. "If I have learned one thing, True, it is that loss comes suddenly. Losing you would be a wound I could never heal, but there would be some small comfort in having your child still."

"To raise alone?"

"To hold near my heart."

"Then do not weep. We are together now, and surely you know I am, as ever, at your command."

"Then with every sun that rises and each one that sets, I command you to stay."

****

"I know who you are."

The words came softly from Pith—an uncanny echo of those which Tally had spoken—as True helped the old man up from his bed in the frosty morning. They'd kept the habit of this, True coming to lend his assistance after he and Barta rose. He and Pith usually talked of little things like the weather or what might be in the breakfast pot. True hadn't expected this admission.

He paused and gave Pith a stare. The journey east and the rough conditions in successive camps hadn't gone easy with him. Already frail, he'd now dropped weight, and visibly struggled to get around on his own.

Yet his spirit held strong.

His grayed hair hung in a tangle across his face. The blow that had blinded him, taken in that long-ago battle, had left a deep scar and stolen one eye; the other appeared white and unfocused.

But he seemed to regard True for an instant before he smiled. "Why are you so surprised? Should I fail to recognize one who has served me so…loyally?"

True's heart dropped. He stole a measured look over his shoulder to make sure no one was near enough to overhear. First Tally and now Pith—was he undone?

Turning back to Pith, he managed but a single word. "How?"

"Well, boy, you must remember I use all my senses to recognize those with whom I come into contact. I tend to connect with them spirit to spirit, and I sensed something familiar in you almost from the first. I am ashamed to say it took me far longer than it should have to put the pieces in place. But it is such an unlikely thing, I scarcely dared jump to it: a hound transforming into a man."

"Master, please." True went hot with desperation. "She does not know."

"Barta? Well, as I say, no one would easily leap to it. That must have been a tremendous feat of magic. How did you achieve it?"

"I did not. The goddess—"

"Ah. Took pity on you, did she?"

"Yes, Master."

"I wish she'd take pity on me and gift me such a fine strong body in place of this ruined one."

"Master—I cannot tell Barta. Nor can you. I am here only for a time, and if she does not guess it on her own, the spell will break. I will become, once more, a dead hound." In consternation True admitted, "I was certain she would guess at once, as soon as she looked into my eyes."

"Yes, but, boy, it is a steep hill to climb, is it not? Especially for one weighed down by guilt. She sees you as a man, moreover one to whom she is attracted. Difficult to look past that."

"Master, you will not tell?"

"What do you take me for?" Again Pith fixed True with that almost-stare. "Has no one else guessed? It

213

seems so obvious to me now. The pieces were all there. None but one with the endurance of a hound could have won that competition—single-minded and near-impervious to pain. No one but Loyal would have bonded with Barta so quickly nor—as I am told—slept across her door."

"Please, Master, do not use that name!"

Pith grunted. "Who else does know?"

"Master Tally. And I believe Mistress Essa guessed the truth."

"Ah, yes, two very skilled at sensing magic. For, my boy, magic trails you like scent. You do not know how long you have with us?"

"No, Master."

"Then was it wise to lie with Barta? Aye—that news is all over camp also. Was it canny to strengthen your ties in that way and risk breaking her heart?"

"Her heart was broken already when I arrived. I sought only to comfort her. Anyway—I do not suppose either of us could have resisted. The ties of which you speak run deep, deeper even than physical joining."

Pith grunted again, unhappily this time. "Well if you want to keep others from guessing, I have a few suggestions."

"Yes, Master Pith?"

"Be less the hound."

True frowned over it. "How am I to do that, Master?"

"Become more the man—and a man, moreover, invested in your current position. Stop with calling folk 'master' and 'mistress'—they are your equals now. And take your own life into your hands."

"I do not understand, ma—Pith."

"Young men, and particularly young warriors of your ilk, do not always wait to be told what to do. They are masters of their own fates."

"But I have never been my own master." He'd listened to Barta, or any other person who commanded him.

"There is your problem. Self-sacrifice is all well and good, True, particularly in a warrior. But if you want the place at her side, you must become the man she believes you to be."

"How?" True asked again.

"Make a decision or two for yourself. Follow your own desires."

"I am not sure I can. Anyway, her desires are my desires."

"Ha! How intoxicating is that for a woman? No wonder she keeps you at her heels."

"Ma—Pith, you will not tell her?" True swallowed hard. Bad enough having to worry about slips from Tally's tongue, let alone Pith's.

"Nay, but, boy, surely you want her to guess."

"Yes, of course."

"What hints have you given her?"

"Few. I fear the wrong person guessing—and speaking—if I do." True swallowed hard. "That night, when the Lady transformed me, I felt so certain Barta would know me at once, as soon as I reached her and gazed into her eyes. I am still me, you see. The one who ran after her, comforted her tears, stood beside her in battle. Died for her. But at first she would not look into my eyes. And even now when we have been as close as the bodies of two persons can be, she knows me not."

Pith reached out and clapped him on the arm, a

gesture of comfort. "It is a great leap for a woman to make, that a man walking into her life used to run behind her on four paws—perhaps more than you can expect. Have you prayed about it?"

"Prayed, Pith?"

"As you must have done that night you were transformed. I'm guessing you prayed then."

"Yes."

"Sue the god and the goddess for mercy now, boy. Argue Barta's need for you and yours for her. Perhaps you can learn how long you have with us—or win leave to stay for good and all."

"You think so?"

Pith shook his head. "I called on the Lord of all when I was blinded—you can bet I did. He answered me not by restoring my sight but by bestowing on me a measure of other Sight. The gods, boy, do not think the same way as you or I." The old man gave a rueful grin. "Or should I say, like me? I have little knowledge as to how a hound thinks, save seldom of himself."

"Pith, please…"

"No, I will say no more of it. But"—Pith's grip on True's arm tightened—"until you can glean a hint of your future, I would not lie again with Barta."

"Eh?" That only confirmed what he, True, had feared.

"Well, you might lie with her as I suppose hounds and their mistresses do, but I would not…"

"Mate her? So I did tell her. She insists."

"If you leave her with child when the goddess snatches you away, it could prove difficult for her."

"She says a child would prove a comfort and has welcomed my breeding. And I must admit, being with

216

her so is a great comfort to me also."

Pith shrugged. "It is up to you, boy." He gave a small smile. "You can sacrifice for her again. Then again, you just might decide, for the first time in your life, to take what you want."

Chapter Twenty-Seven

"It is cold tonight." Barta snuggled closer to True in their blankets. Though several huts had been raised at this new camp beside the stream, those had been given to the elderly, the infirm, and the very young. She and True lay in the open with nothing overhead but the bare branches of a tree. Past those branches True could glimpse widely flung stars, and the air stung with frost.

He had tried to speak to the goddess that afternoon, after leaving Pith—had gone off by himself and called out to her. He'd won no response. No doubt Pith had it right—all the times he'd called to her and received an answer, he'd been under great duress and suffused with longing. His heart told him it must be thus before he reached her again.

Barta wiggled in his arms and buried her face in his neck. He recalled doing the same to her when he was her hound and wished, in the night, to gather her scent.

Now, though, her movement only served to arouse him. He recalled Pith's words of caution and strove to rein in his emotions.

"Hold me," Barta requested. "Closer. You know just how close I want to be."

He did. Moreover, so did that part of him which served to link them in such pleasure. He sighed; this looked to prove a difficult night.

"What is it?" To be sure, near as she was to him

Barta could feel his discomfort. "I thought you loved it when we are together."

"So I do—" He got no further, for she slid her tongue into his mouth. Oh, most glorious sensation! He loved her, yes, from her head to her toes and especially this well of wild flavor when she desired him.

As a hound he'd lived always and ever for the moment. Must that change?

She wiggled again, mouth fused to his, and he felt her unfasten the ties on her tunic. Suddenly he wanted her breast in his mouth, desired it more than breathing. He wanted the strength and completeness that came when he slid into her. But...

He broke the kiss to say, "Barta, do you think you carry my child?"

"Is that why your hesitate? It is well, True; folks continue to make love together even when the child becomes great; it harms nothing."

Not like hounds, then. The few bitches he'd successfully bred wanted nothing to do with him when not in heat and snarled if he came after them.

Barta definitely did not snarl—she caressed his face with her fingers and plunged them into his hair.

He struggled to retain control of his thoughts. "But—do you?"

"Think I'm carrying your child? No, not yet. Of course I can't be certain. Why do you ask?"

"If you have my child, that will make it that much harder for me if I must leave you."

"That, again?" She yelped the words and stiffened in his arms. "I thought I told you, you are not allowed to leave me. Promise you will not!"

"I cannot give that promise. It is a very real

possibility—I might be recalled at any time."

"Yes but—so much has happened since you were sent to me. The contest, the destruction of the settlement…the loss of my parents. Our love for one another. Surely that changes everything?"

"I fear not. Were it up to me, Barta, I would never leave you. It is not up to me."

She thought on that with an intensity he felt. "There must be a way."

"I have tried to think of one. The spell that holds me—that allowed me to come here—might dissolve at any time." *Unless you guess who I am,* he added silently.

"Unbearable." She huffed the word. "It seems as if I have known you and loved you forever. How could I hope to endure losing you?"

He had no answer for that and remained silent. He felt her thoughts rushing.

At last she said, "But it is as I told you before: should that dire event occur, I can imagine no greater joy than having your child with me for always."

"Barta…"

"Do you mean to tell me you intend never to make love to me again? Even when we lie together like this?"

Make love, as he knew very well, was what she called breeding. But it remained breeding, all the same.

"It would break my heart," he told her, "to leave both you and my child."

"I had not thought of that. Am I being selfish again? True, I've tried so hard to change."

"You are perfect just the way you are. Perfect." He licked her cheek, and she turned her head so their open mouths met once more, tongues tangling. This time when she broke the kiss they were both breathless.

"Surely, though, one more time won't hurt," she wooed.

He wondered. A hound, he nonetheless wore the body of a man, compatible with hers. Yet might it be possible he could not successfully breed her? Might the goddess have lent that protection against their eventual parting?

But there were so few protections in the world.

Barta whimpered, "We can do it the way you like best, like beasts."

He quickened still farther and groaned. He did prefer her in that position, though front to front allowed him access to her beautiful mouth.

"I will take you," she breathed, "any way you desire."

Ah, and was this an opportunity to seize the autonomy Pith recommended? Should he impose his will on hers? A shocking prospect.

"Or," she continued when he did not respond, "we might do it all the ways we've tried so far, one after another. You decide."

He smiled wryly despite the fierce ache of his desire. "And if I decide not to breed you this night?"

"Breed me? That's an odd term for lovemaking."

"That's what it is, Barta."

"If you would withhold yourself from me, that's your right. I do not command you." She slid her hands downward from his hair, over his shoulders, around to his chest, and lower still. Her fingers wrapped around the hot, heavy length of him. "But why would you decide such a thing when we have a whole, long night ahead?"

Why, indeed?

He growled deep in his throat. If he must decide, he would choose as he always had—for the moment. Tomorrow would come, or it would not.

He turned her over beneath him, with gentle hands.

Chapter Twenty-Eight

"I say we should go back. Today—before the weather worsens and while we stand the best chance of reclaiming our land."

Tally's voice still sounded like that of a mere boy, but Barta had to admit he looked far more. A new strength had come upon her young brother and enfolded him like an invisible cloak.

He would need all his strength, she acknowledged, facing off against a scowling Brude in the morning light. Brude, too, appeared to have aged, the weight of his new responsibilities scoring lines into his forehead.

They stood in two decided factions, facing each other: Brude's supporters and Tally's. The tribe, as Barta had feared, was very nearly sundered in two, the last thing her father would have wanted and the last thing they needed now, when they were so few in number.

Brude, with his height and bulk of muscle, might make two of Tally, yet the boy stood straight as a spear and looked the other man in the eyes, awaiting his response.

Brude, in the past always quick to speak his mind, seemed to weigh his words before delivering them, standing with Avinda at his side and a number of the young warriors at his back.

"We will not make a challenge this season.

Mayhap in the spring."

"Says who?" Tally challenged.

"Says I," Brude told him sourly.

"But you are not chief of this tribe. Not rightful chief," Tally returned swiftly. "You stepped into the place merely because there was no one else. The rightful chief should be Wick, or failing him, me. Failing me, my sister's son."

"Your brother, whelp, has scuttled away, and your sister has no son. As for you—you are but a pup."

Tally's chin lifted still further. "One with a chief's blood in his veins."

Barta exchanged a look with True, with whom she stood shoulder to shoulder, their fingers linked. Nearly a fortnight had passed since the evening he'd agreed to make love to her, and they'd scarcely been apart. The deep wound in her heart, so she believed, had nearly closed beneath the balm of his presence and love.

She glanced at the others who stood with them while they waited for Brude's reply: Gant just behind her, stolid and sure; Gede behind him, Rekka and her friends at Tally's side.

Barta recognized that deep ties had also developed between Rekka and Tally. Had they already lain together? Yet her brother had barely fifteen winters.

And had been forced to grow up overnight. Her fingers twitched in True's. Who was she to question?

True caressed her fingers comfortingly. She steadied where she stood.

"Our past," Brude told Tally and the listening crowd, "has been swept away. I say the man best fit to lead must step into the place. And I am best fit to lead."

"Are you?" Tally challenged. "Are you indeed? I

say that is for the tribe as a whole to decide."

"Yet, whelp, the tribe is no longer whole. You have managed to break it apart with your interfering. Now you would take a broken tribe to challenge the Gaels who may well be dug in back there, even as we are here."

Pith stepped forward from behind Tally. "I am the oldest of us left alive," he declared in his quavering voice, "and I have consulted with the gods on this matter. You can see where I stand—with Radoc's family. The rest of you must make your own choices."

The crowd buzzed as people muttered to one another. Brude's dark eyes narrowed abruptly.

"Why, old man? Why do you wish to go back there and die?"

"And who are you, Brude map Edder, to question my ties to our land or my loyalty?"

Brude drew himself up indignantly even as Avinda shot him a look. "I question nothing. But land is land, and life is life. You all know me—I am the last to run. Yet winter is upon us. I say we gather our strength and hit the Gaels in the spring."

"Winter is the secret season," Tally declared, sounding so much like his mother Barta had to close her eyes a moment against a rush of memory and pain. "It is time for us who know this land to act. The Gaels will try and hold what they have stolen, yes. They will dig in and set a stout guard. But as we know from past experience, they will halt their battling—which is exactly why we should not. A series of hit-and-run raids, carried out mostly at night, with the forest to shield us—that is how we will defeat them."

More murmuring, a rising current this time. Folk

put their heads together even while Brude sneered. "Yes—because the last of our night-time raids worked so well, that your sister launched—that which began all this hurt and misery."

Ah, thought Barta, was she never to live that down, even though she'd paid such a high price, her life shaken to its very roots?

True squeezed her fingers again as if he sensed her spike of agitation.

Tally refused to rise to Brude's jibe. "My sister carries my father's courage. That is why I propose she should act as head of our tribal war council."

He got no farther. Even as Barta stiffened in shock, Brude lost the last of his stern self-control and bellowed, "Her? To lead us? Into disaster and more death, say I!"

"You may say what you will, Brude map Edder. I do not suggest my sister for war chief but as leader of a group that will include you and many others, to make decisions jointly."

"You expect me to take advice from that traitorous vixen? I would sooner crawl into my own grave."

"Now who threatens to sunder us?" Tally retorted. "We must all—all—work together if we are to succeed. If we keep retreating—"

"As your brother has?" Brude sneered. "Why do you not accuse him of cowardice, rather than me?"

"I do not accuse you of cowardice, Brude map Edder. Far from it. That is why I want you on my side. My brother, Wick, will find his heart and return. Master Pith and I have both Seen it. Meanwhile, Radoc's house still stands. I am here to tell you so."

Pride flooded Barta's heart. Tally indeed embodied

the best of both their parents.

She stepped forward, pulling her fingers from True's. "And I."

"I." Gant moved to her shoulder.

"I." Gede with a grunt.

"And I." Now Pith's voice did not quaver.

Brude stood confounded, his face thunderous.

Quietly, Tally spoke to the tribe's folk rather than Brude. "Go you off and consider on this thing. Consult with your gods, your hearts, and one another. We will meet here again at nightfall, and you will give me—and Brude—your decisions."

The crowd moved off slowly, Brude one of the last to leave, an ugly look in his eyes.

****

"Do you truly believe Wick will return?" Barta asked her brother hopefully.

True, who sat beside her, glanced into her face. They and several others had gathered around a small fire that did little to battle the chill. True could not see the position of the sun—low cloud cover prevented it—but he guessed sunset could not be far off.

Last night the first snowflakes had fallen. Had that been what prompted Tally's bold stand, a prick from the spear of winter?

And was Tally right, calling for a return to their old lands, an attempt to reclaim them? True wished he knew, wished he could look ahead and see what would happen, how long the Lady would allow him to stay.

As if she felt his agitation, Barta slid her hand over his knee just the way she used to caress his head when he was a hound.

"I told Brude no lie," Tally replied softly. "I have

Seen it."

"And do you supposed Brude will join with us if the tribe decides to go back?" Barta pressed. "Tally, you should not have placed me at the head of a war council. Brude will never agree to take orders from me. And we need his spear."

"Then, Sister, you must find a way to get along with him. Trot out some of Mother's tact, if you can."

Gant smothered a laugh. "Tact? Barta? Tally, are you sure your wits have all returned to you?"

They all laughed but uneasily.

Rekka spoke up then. "I am proud of Tally."

"And I."

"I."

"I."

The avowals traveled around the fire, swift and fervent. Barta and Tally exchanged a heartfelt glance; it should have been a good moment, but for an instant foreboding gripped True's heart. Just as if he had suddenly been granted the ability he'd wished for, to see ahead, he knew the tribe would decide to stand behind Tally, that they would be called upon to fight.

They would make a journey into darkness.

There beside the quiet fire, he caught his breath, knowing he would travel even into that darkness, so long as it be at Barta's side.

Chapter Twenty-Nine

A cold wind teased the back of Barta's neck, sending chilly fingers through her clothing and down her spine. Snow stung one cheek and obscured what she could see of the Gaels' settlement through the trees.

She could feel the others of her party all around her—True as ever on her left hand, the rest of their warriors, including Brude, silent as the trees. At her signal, an owl's call, they would move—the third such raid launched in a seven-night.

The first two had been wildly successful, far more so than she could have hoped. This would be harder— the Gaels expected them now and had set a strong guard around the camp that used to be the Epidii's own.

But even the most vigilant guard flagged in the pit of the night when the wind blew coldest, and Barta's band could move very quietly indeed. As during the first two raids, they had their targets chosen—they would fell any guards they met before freeing the Gaels' ponies and damaging their chariots.

The Gaels would not last the winter here. If they did, they would have to fight without their accursed carts, come spring.

She narrowed her eyes when she caught movement just ahead—a member of the Gaels' guard walking his line. Far too predictable were these westerners, and she could smell his stink from here. No matter; he would be

229

the first to die by her blade.

She heard True begin to pant beside her, and for an instant her grasp on reality wavered—time shifted and she thought she waited to enter the battle with Loyal at her side.

She shivered. A bad omen?

Surely not. The illusion of Loyal's company could only give her strength.

She threw back her head and gave the owl's cry. As silently as that bird in flight, her party moved forward through the trees.

****

"A great victory and no mistake." Brude's face shone with savage joy as he made the declaration.

So it was, and Barta could have chortled over it. For once everything seemed to be going the way of the Epidii. The Gaelic guard she'd earmarked had gone down—silently—to her blade. They'd stolen four ponies and destroyed a raft of chariots before slipping away, without losing a single man. Oh, they'd taken injuries—True, as she knew, had suffered two—but none too grave. And for the first time, as they stood around their own fire celebrating, even Brude seemed to have embraced the plan.

Barta eyed True, who bore a slash to one arm—not yet tended—and who lapped uncertainly at his cup of heather ale. No secret that he did not much like the taste of ale and would sooner have water.

But a celebration must include ale, and they did celebrate over the victory behind them—even gloated just a bit as the sun rose.

"The Gaels may follow us," Gede proposed, a caution.

"They might well try," Gant declared. "They cannot move as easily as we do through the forest, nor as quietly. They may try and track the ponies we loosed, but most of those scattered. I say bad luck to them."

Barta met True's gaze—bright hazel filled with golden lights—and knew what dominated his thoughts. Following each successful raid so far they'd made wild, passionate love fueled by the rush still coursing through their veins.

"Come, let us get that arm of yours tended," she told him and towed him away by the hand, only half aware of the knowing smiles that followed them.

Had the tribe's folk accepted True at last? Certainly he could not be more valiant in battle or less stinting in risking his own safety.

Before they even reached the edge of the trees where the Epidii hid their mobile camp, True dragged her to a halt and turned her to face him.

"Do you in truth mean to tend my arm?"

Breathless she answered, "That wound needs care."

"Later, mayhap."

"Better at once. I want to put on some of that salve I made—not as good as Mother's but better than nothing. I know how strong you are, True, but poisoning can so easily set in…"

"Later," he repeated. "I want you first. Want you, Barta."

Her bones promptly turned molten. "I want you too. But it will take only a moment. I have the salve here at our bedside."

"Hush."

Barta went silent with surprise. Seldom did True

order her to anything; rarely did he impose his will over hers. And what did she see in his eyes? Certainty, and a new confidence burning through the rampant desire.

"The arm will take care of itself," he told her with emphasis. "I will take care of you."

"Yes." She did not consciously move forward into his arms, merely fell into the sense of belonging that always swamped her there, the heat of his mouth and the weight of him pressed against her. She wrapped her arms around his neck and her legs around his waist, mouths joined irresistibly. He carried her so through the misty trees to their bedroll, where he laid her gently.

Hazy and half mad with desire, she lay gazing up at him while he removed his clothing, revealing that long, lean-muscled body she'd come to know so well. Her mouth began to water.

"True…"

"Have I not told you to hush?" Affection spilled from him.

"I merely want to tell you how beautiful I think you are."

He came down on top of her and began to unfasten her clothing. "I think you are the most beautiful person ever to walk on the face of the world." His hands moved tenderly, dispensing with her tunic, uncovering her breasts. "But if you were not—if you had a scar across your face and had lost an eye, mayhap, like Pith—I would still love you and would still follow you."

Barta's heart clenched in her chest. "Oh, True."

"Do you know why, Barta?"

Barta shook her head helplessly; she couldn't imagine. With all her faults, how could she be worthy of this beautiful man's company? Of his devotion?

"Because the bond between us is so strong."

"Yes. Love me, True, please."

He did, slowly at first and with attention that neglected no part of her before fire consumed the both of them together, the act so beautiful that when they lay spent in one another's arms, tears flooded Barta's eyes.

She wondered again what miracle had brought him to her, this stranger come out of a dark night with no past and barely a promise of a future, but bearing so much in his graceful hands—strength, devotion, and loyalty only ever matched by one other being.

"Tell me," she whispered as he lay still inside her in the most intimate of unions, his cheek pressed against hers. "Tell me from whence you came."

"I cannot, Barta. Do not ask me."

"Then tell me what you know of the future. Sometimes when we sit in council with the others making our plans, I catch a look in your eyes…"

"What look, Mistress?"

"As if you know how long we will have together."

He hesitated a moment before he spoke. "I do not. I know only that I want to be with you, I am with you, and that is enough. Live in the moment, Barta, and be satisfied."

"That has never been easy for me."

"But you are strong enough to accomplish it, to accomplish anything."

"I am not strong enough to survive losing you. Anything else, True."

He drew a breath. "I always told you I may not have leave to stay. I warned you of that again and again, when we spoke of a child. You said—"

233

"I know what I said. But now winter is upon us, and I'm looking for eternity. I'm a selfish creature, after all. I want reassurance so I can face today and tomorrow, and all the days to come."

"I cannot give you that assurance. Only my love. It will be yours always and forever—so long as my heart beats and even when it stills once more."

"Once more?" She drew away far enough to look into his eyes. At such close quarters, with the shaggy hair falling across his brow, he barely looked like a man at all, but somehow familiar for all that. "What do you mean, once more?"

"Have we not all lived many times? Do our spirits not come and go like the seasons, donning new bodies like new tunics? So the gods do teach."

"You think we knew each other before?" And would that explain the sense of familiarity that dogged her?

"I know it."

"Ah." She eased slightly. "But such partings come with age. Surely we will have many seasons." She knew, given the lives they now lived, age could not be promised. But she voiced the wish like a prayer against the unknown.

"I will make you a promise, True—here and now I will: I lay aside all my selfishness, all my self-interest and my headstrong complaints—for your sake. You come first with me, best and last. And I will trade anything for your company. Do you think the gods are listening?"

"They are always listening."

"Do you suppose they will, then, permit you to stay with me?"

"I cannot say."

Earnestly she told him—and told the gods—"I will be a different woman, a better woman, for your sake."

"I cannot imagine you being better than you are."

"Oh, True." The tears in her eyes spilled over. "Then I ask but one thing of you."

"Anything, Barta."

"Before the next raid, wed with me."

Chapter Thirty

Among the Epidii, handfastings customarily took place at the beginning of winter. Then was the fighting done for the season; then were hearth fires bright. Folk turned their minds from survival to begetting the next generation.

As Barta stood beside True with her hand in his and all the remaining members of the tribe looking on, she wondered again whether she might already be carrying. Part of her hoped so—she longed for True's child so much she ached. But such a state would lend her vulnerability in battle that she couldn't afford. For they planned many more raids in the months to come.

One this very night.

She raised her eyes and studied the beloved faces that surrounded her. So very much had changed since True's arrival. Her parents—gone, along with so many friends. Tally standing with a new gravity upon him. Brude aged so swiftly, hand in hand with Avinda, who wore a serious expression. Gant—but yes, Gant looked pleased for her, as did Pith, his face creased in a smile.

As for True—her intended husband, her lover, her very reason for drawing breath...

She turned to face him and placed her other hand in his. Their gazes met, and for an instant she lost all her breath. She felt as if her heart might burst.

How could it be that they'd been together only

since the start of autumn? It must be as he'd said, they'd shared a past life, for everything about him spoke to her of comfort and familiarity so deep it sounded to her core. His bright eyes, full of devotion, never wavered from hers as she spoke.

"Now am I yours: wife, friend, and helpmate, from this moment to the end of my life."

His fingers tightened on hers, and gladness lit him from within. He repeated the vow gravely, "Now am I yours, husband, friend, and helpmate, from this moment to the end of my life."

"A heart gifted, a life sworn."

"A heart gifted, a life sworn."

Barta, who never bent to any man—had never expected to—bowed her head and lifted his hands one after the other to her lips. Love and devotion together flooded her in a wave so strong it nearly took her to her knees.

But no, for True was there to uplift her. The strength of his hands, still fast on hers, bore her upward, and a few cheers sounded from the crowd.

"Kiss her!" someone called—it might have been Gede. True drew Barta to him, and their lips met with exquisite tenderness there before the tribe, declaring them one.

Barta closed her eyes at the sheer pleasure of it, breaking contact with True's gaze at last, and felt the fullness of their connection. From now on she lived for him—his needs, his well-being before her own.

For an instant, eyes still closed, she thought she felt a cold tear on her cheek. His? Hers? She opened her eyes to find snowflakes dancing all around them, keeping time with the music in her heart.

****

"This raid," Tally announced, "will be our most important yet." He stood straight and tall at the center of the warriors ready to set out into the night. The snow that had whirled down so playfully when True and Barta stood plighting their devotion—a thing True had no real need to profess—now made a small blizzard through which they would have to travel to reach the Gaels' encampment, formerly their own.

He narrowed his eyes and focused on young Master Tally, his attention still more than half centered on the woman beside him. The bond between them had strengthened to a level of constant awareness. He knew when she breathed, when she thought of him.

He could feel her love, and it colored his world.

But Tally—when had the boy grown to his sister's height? From whence had he gained such poise?

"We have them nearly flighted, chased from our ancestral lands. Only a few ponies left, many injured warriors. They will not expect us to hit them out of this storm. But"—Tally drew himself up still farther—"we are of this land—and so part of the wind and the very snow."

Those listening, a band some half score strong that included Gant, Gede, and Brude, nodded.

Tally went on, "A powerful magic accompanies us this night. May your spears be sharp, your blades keen. Slay all you may. You take the means for fire with you—put the rest to flame. May the god and goddess watch over us all."

Many in the band repeated the last words, a charm for safety and a blessing, before they began to move off.

Tally called, "Sister, a word before you go."

Barta paused and True, perforce, with her. Tally stepped up, and True saw that in truth the lad nearly topped his sister.

"What is it, Brother? We must leave at once if we are to hit them in the depths of the night."

"Yes, but I wished to say—I have Seen this is to be a pivotal battle. I did not want to tell the others and so color their expectations, but if we can win this, we can chase them. Then we will raise a grand round tower on the site where our ancestors lie. A fortress."

Barta stared at him in amazement. "Are you certain of this?"

"I am." Tally, his eyes troubled, drew a breath. "That being said, there is danger also—sharp as a whetted blade." His gaze moved to True and back again. "You do not have to take part in this foray. It is your wedding night—"

"And," Barta told him swiftly, "I am a woman changed—transformed by my husband's love. Surely, Brother, you understand that."

"I do. Yet the peril is deep, especially for the two of you."

"And if we do not participate, if we stay here all warm and safe in our bed, Tally, the Epidii may not prove victorious."

"That is so. But perhaps, Sister, you should consult with your husband before you make this decision for him."

True spoke before Barta could. "I go whence she goes, Master Tally. That I know you above all others understand."

Tally merely bit his lip and nodded. To True's

surprise, the boy stepped forward and embraced him, arms clutching hard before he turned to his sister and hugged her also, most fiercely.

"The gods go with you on your way."

"What did you mean by that?" Barta asked True as they walked off.

"By what, Wife?"

"That Tally, above all others, should understand why you accompany me."

True shook his head. "Mere words, Barta. You know how difficult they are for me."

****

It seemed Tally had been wrong after all when he gave them warning. All went far too well; the snow swirling dense and dizzying held the Gaels' camp in its fist and screened the Epidii's approach perfectly. The guards neither saw nor heard them; taken out silently, they fell one by one, the last to Barta's own blade. Not until they went to free the remaining ponies did the first part of their plan go awry; the beasts, confined and huddled against the weather, stood where they were and refused to be chased off.

Then Brude and Gede had trouble striking a light to fire the chariots. By the time Barta, with True at her side, ran to help them, the alarm had been given. Gaels streamed from their shelters on every hand. The battle became fierce and personal.

Opponents seemed to appear and disappear through the snow—a blade here, a contorted visage there—and shouts rang through the frigid air.

Barta stood back-to-back with True, a fighting stance the Epidii often employed so no opponent could attack from behind. So close were they she could feel the muscles of his shoulders flex, could almost sense his flash of victory when he took his opponents down. But they seemed isolated in the night, with the shrieking, hollering Gaels coming at them from every side. Where were the rest of the Epidii? Barta could hear them fighting not far off but could catch no glimpse.

Then she saw flames flare as someone succeeded in setting the chariots alight, no doubt with the help of the grease they'd brought. Victory flared in her heart, and she edged around, her back still to True's, to face her next opponent. They would finish this thing now, chase these vermin from Epidii soil—she would avenge her parents this night.

She bared her teeth and hauled up her blade. Before her eyes appeared a countenance she recognized—fiercely twisted and surrounded by flying yellow hair.

The leader of the Gaels—he who had directed this campaign against them, stolen their lands, moved against her friends...

Who had murdered Loyal.

She screamed with hatred and glee—here then stood her chance for revenge and victory all in one, to be seized at a blow. Before her stood their enemies' heart.

He'd been wounded in one of their past encounters, perhaps the same one that had seen Loyal fall. Now he fixed his gaze on Barta as if he saw nothing else and raised a blade already stained with blood.

Whose blood? She had time to wonder nothing more before he launched himself at her and she embarked on the fight of her life.

Her blade—also red—met his in a grating grind she felt in her clenched teeth. His sword had greater length than her long knife and more power behind it. Yet he could not drive her back because True, behind her and also fighting, stood like a rock.

One blow, two—she fended off the Gaels' leader and wondered how she was to best him. Another three crashing strikes from his blade and she feared she was in danger—Tally's warning flashed through her mind and dissipated in her desperation. She felt...

True's entire body reacted as he suffered a blow. Horror suffused her and fear far more intense than that for her own safety. He was struck! Ah, goddess, no—it could not happen.

Not again.

The horror gave her strength enough to launch herself at her opponent and momentarily throw him over.

She turned, as did True, he having apparently vanquished his enemy. She saw his pain-wracked face, wide eyes, and lower, the terrible slash that ran in a diagonal across his chest, opening his tunic and the skin beneath. Blood already welled there, but he spared it no heed. Instead he leaped to her with a fierce growl.

Just as the Gaelic leader seized Barta from behind and yanked her against him, his blade at her throat.

Chapter Thirty-One

True, still panting hard from the fight just behind him, squinted and strove desperately to see through the swirling snow. No mistaking the scene—a tall man with a wild mop of yellow hair and a face contorted by hate held Barta fast against him, the stained blade of his sword hard at her vulnerable throat.

For an instant reality wavered; True flashed back to a similar scene, another place. The same man's face and fierce demeanor—this person had swung his blade at Barta then also. Loyal had leaped in front of her and knocked her down. The blade had taken him, Loyal, instead. He'd fallen and covered Barta's body with his own. The last thing he'd seen had been this man's face as he drew Loyal's head back to cut his throat, making sure he would rise no more.

Yet he'd arisen—with the help of the goddess— and had a chance for revenge. A chance he could not take if it endangered Barta. And it would.

Ignoring the wound slashed across his chest, he snarled again and met the gaze of the Gael who held Barta in a fierce grip. At that moment it seemed only the three of them existed. The snow still swirled down, and at a distance True could hear the cries of the dying, the victorious whoops from the Epidii tribe's men. But what good a victory if Barta—the ruling star of True's life—should be slain? One wrong move on his part and her life would end as had Loyal's, by the same blade.

Tearing his gaze from the Gael's, he looked into Barta's eyes. He would gladly trade his life for hers again. He did not know how.

The Gael, wordless in his intentions, drew her more brutally against him. Then he threw back his head and emitted a shocking sound—a piercing whistle that cut through the storm.

At first there seemed no response; then, out of the darkness exploded a pony, one that must have refused to run. Shaggy gray it was, with a wild eye.

True spun to face it even as it tossed its head, dancing with alarm. The Gael spoke to it—called to it—in his own tongue, and despite its distress it came to him.

True edged closer, looking for a way to take advantage and get Barta free, but her captor shouted at him also and made a gesture with his sword that had Barta grimacing in pain.

True's heart swelled with agony. His every muscle and sinew wanted to leap. Instinct bade him to caution. He could not risk Barta's life.

The Gael hollered at him again before edging himself and Barta against the pony. In an incredible show of strength the man leaped onto the pony's naked back, dragging Barta with him.

"No!" The protest came from True in a bark. This happened too swiftly; his choices were too few. Even as he leaped toward them the Gael, commanding the pony with his knees, bounded away. True had time to meet Barta's panicked gaze—no more—before they charged off into the swirling snow westward.

With a snarl he threw down his long knife—he'd

already broken his spear some time during the fight. He had still his dirk thrust into the loop on the side of his boot, and that would have to suffice.

Once he caught them.

The other ponies had scattered, and he had more faith, anyhow, in his own limbs. He scented the air, knowing he would need to rely on every sense in order to follow, and found Gant at his side.

"Victorious! We are victorious!" Gant's face, sweaty despite the chill, shone. "Where is Barta?"

"Gone. The Gael leader took her." Words very nearly deserted True in his rage. "Must follow."

"Wait—we will all come. Let me rally the others."

"They are on horseback. Dare not lose them."

"But, man"—Gant seized True's arm and his gaze dropped to True's chest—"you're sore wounded."

"Let me go." They were the last words True wasted. He shook free from Gant's grasp and pelted off in the direction Barta and her captor had ridden, only Gant's cry of protest following behind.

****

Barta's captor stank. Or perhaps it was the reek of her own fear that flooded her nostrils—with the two of them pressed together so tightly, she could barely tell. She knew her body had been drenched with sweat that dried quickly as they rode into the cold dark.

She could smell other things as well—the sharp fragrance of the fire behind them, the scent of the pony. And blood.

Was her captor wounded? Was she? She tried to take stock of her physical condition and failed. She could feel only her heart beating suffocatingly up in her throat and what might be a trickle of moisture from the place where the Gael had previously pressed his blade.

She could see only the expression in True's eyes as she'd been hauled up onto the pony. She'd seen that same look before—she knew she had. The circumstances—danger and pain—had been very nearly the same. But...

With sudden, blinding clarity the answer came. Loyal.

True's eyes and Loyal's were the same.

Why had she never realized that before? Because Loyal was a hound and True a man.

Wasn't he?

And now with each pound of the pony's hooves she moved farther and farther away from him. Every part of her protested that. And she could feel...

The bond between them stretching, drawing out painfully. But never breaking.

Never.

She caught her breath in wonder at the thought possessing her mind.

Impossible. And yet...

He'd told her from the beginning he'd been through a great transformative experience. That magic had sent him. And she believed to the root of her soul that magic could accomplish anything.

Yet now he'd been left far behind her. She found herself in the very clutches of peril with no means to ask True for the truth.

Dared she try and break free, to run back to him who, in any form, possessed her heart? For she knew herself linked with him—spirit to spirit. The rest was just the clothing they wore.

She shifted in her captor's arms, and he grunted at

her. He had put away his sword and held a dirk clutched in his fist instead—a sharp, nasty thing she knew could end her life in the wink of an eye. He wanted safe away; she was his hostage.

She tried to fight through her tangled emotions and think clearly. So very often in the past she'd acted too swiftly and foolishly. But she'd learned better. The costs could be unbearably high.

But where might this savage take her besides away into the night? Would he drag her all the way to Dal Riada, where she would spend her life as a slave?

Would he slit her throat as soon as he thought himself far enough away?

But…her inner knowing told her that might not be so easy as he believed. For she could feel quite distinctly the cord that bound her to True vibrating. And that told her he followed.

How? Surely not on foot—he'd been sore injured. Had he caught one of the other ponies?

It did not matter; he came.

"He follows after us," she told her captor in her own tongue. Would he understand?

He grunted again and grated into her ear, also in her language, "Who does?"

"My mate."

"He will not catch us. And if he does, he will then watch you die."

Oh, True, oh, True—my love. Have a care, my love.

Chapter Thirty-Two

True's breath scorched his lungs, every gasp like fire. The slash across his chest, though not deep, nevertheless seeped blood steadily, draining his strength. How long had he followed the pony with its precious burden? He could not tell; he had little orientation amidst the blowing snow and darkness. He followed by sheer instinct, nearly blind.

The brilliant cord that bound him to Barta stretched far but held tight. He found if he narrowed his gaze against the darkness and pain he could glimpse it. That made it easier to follow even than the faint scent of pony and the reek of the westerner.

He cursed as he ran—lamented the limitations of this body in which he found himself. Four paws, as he knew, were swifter than two feet. A hound's deep lungs could gather more air. And a hound's endurance surpassed that of a man. His body might be as fit as that of any person, but he could already feel it flagging. Some while back he'd begun substituting will for strength and knew his condition would only worsen.

A pony carrying double, especially through the dark and storm, should be easy for a hound to catch. As it was, he kept up but doubted he could close the distance between them.

Not but he was willing to die trying. He had died for Barta before and would again. Did she know he followed? He believed so and hoped it gave her heart.

Where might the man with the yellow hair take her? Surely not all the way to the Gaels' far western settlement? If not—if he kept hold of her only until he believed himself safe away and then slit her throat...

True gulped more air, his heart near bursting. He could not bear it; he did not want to live in the world without her. He saw suddenly what a gift it had been for him to die first, the last time. But no, for his heartbreak at their separation, his longing for her, hadn't ended with death. Wasn't that what had put him here now?

He dug deeper for strength, commanded his failing limbs to serve him, and ran on.

Barta, Mistress, wife, can you feel me? Do you know I follow after you?

No response but he fancied the cord between them once more flared bright.

Please, Lady, he prayed to the goddess, only let the pony falter before I do.

****

"We need to let the pony rest."

Barta's captor spoke her language in an ugly burr, its music lost, but yes, she could understand him.

He drew up the pony, which blew and huffed, and wrestled Barta from its back, never once loosening his grip on her.

She strained to look back the way they had come but of course could see nothing.

"Does he get closer, this mate of yours?" The blond Gael was all too aware, too astute. His eyes gleamed at Barta, and he bared his teeth in a vicious smile. "I suppose I cannot kill you yet."

"Is that what you mean to do—kill me?" Barta

despised herself for asking, but her heart thumped in her chest, and she thought of True. She would not want him to risk himself just to stumble over her corpse.

Her captor shrugged, answer enough. She wondered if his grasp of her language allowed for more. His kind had plenty of Caledonii slaves, which they called blue men. They would, however, expect those slaves to learn their tongue.

She shuddered. Surely death would be preferable to servitude. At least then her spirit would fly over the land, over the water and enter bliss.

Or—tethered to True's spirit—would it?

"Let me go," she said, "and he who follows may spare your life."

Her captor laughed in scorn. "A great warrior, is he?"

"The greatest. And he possesses magic—enough to defeat you."

"Magic." He spat the word.

"Do you not believe?" Could he be so foolish?

"I believe in magic." He bared his teeth again. "But what makes you suppose I don't possess it also? I am the man bold and blessed enough to have conquered so much territory east of Dal Riada. I shall be the one to defeat your people and claim all this land as my own."

"Defeat? That outpost back there just fell to my men."

"Your men? Commanded by a woman?" His gaze raked her from her hair downward. "Is it that to which the blue savages must resort in the face of our swords and chariots?"

"Your chariots lie burned."

"We can build more. And we will return."

Barta jerked up her chin. "If you do, you will find a grand fortress. We will not surrender our ancestors' lands twice."

"You have put up a good resistance, I grant you that—better than any we met farther west. But you will fall just like all the others."

He eyed her again, this time with speculation. "There is more than one way to conquer. I've had blue men's women before, of course, but they were all slaves. I've never enjoyed one who thought herself a warrior." He glanced about. "Amid a storm."

The breath stuck in Barta's throat. Would such a vile act delay them long enough for True to catch up? Did she want him to catch up? If he did, would he then fall to this man's blade?

She could almost feel True's heart beating as he followed after her. Wounded—exhausted—would he be in any condition for the fight of his life?

****

True's heart foundered in his chest. How far had he run? Impossible to tell. He could still feel Barta somewhere ahead of him in the night, the cord that bound them glowing like a guiding light. How far ahead? Also impossible to tell.

Now a mist hung before his eyes, obscuring his vision, and pain held him in a deadly grip. His lungs could no longer reach for air; his legs trembled beneath him.

The terrain underfoot sloped upward—because of the snow he could not see how far, but the gradient further taxed muscles already spent.

He stumbled.

Do not let me fall.

To whom did he pray? To the goddess, to the night, to Barta herself. To the ties between them, holy and magical.

If he fell, he doubted he could get up again. And he would not allow himself to fail her; he refused to fail their love.

The wound across his chest still bled. Pain there mingled with that in his heart, which suddenly contracted and nearly brought him to his knees, forcing him to slow for the first time.

A pony, as he knew, could be run to death, as could a hound. A man?

Gasping for breath, he shook his head. As a hound, with greater endurance, he would have a much better chance.

Struggling mightily, he forced his body on. The slope of the hill increased, and when he reached the top his legs gave out beneath him. He went down.

It felt as if the hard ground came up to meet him, all frost and stones. He lay as fallen, cheek pressed against the rubble, desperate for breath that would not come. The shining cord tugged at him, demanded that he rise. But as if his spirit no longer commanded this body, he could not obey.

The snow swirled around him, the wind came and blew over. A bleak and lonely place to die. But he would not allow himself to die and fail Barta.

Using the last of his will, he picked up his head and howled at the sky—he hollered his pain the way he had the night he'd given his life for Barta's, when the goddess answered him.

Would she answer now?

Nothing and no one answered—just the wind in his

ears and the cold creeping in. He could no longer see, and could barely move. Paralysis seemed to creep from his head downward; his chest burned.

"Poor hound." A gentle touch on his head that almost felt like Barta's.

He stiffened in every limb, yearning, wishing he could see, but his vision had failed him.

Someone knelt at his side, her touch a balm. She didn't smell like Barta, whose scent he would know anywhere.

The goddess, then? Yes, for he could sense her light, like that of the moon, embracing and warming him.

Please, he thought.

"Here, hound," she replied calmly, "our venture has gone badly. You made a fine man, but your heart remained that of a hound."

"My heart is my heart and will never change."

"That is your greatest strength as well as your greatest weakness. Look what has come of my boon. You are dying after all."

"Please. Save me again."

"Why should I? For her sake?"

"Everything is for her sake."

"But she is wayward and headstrong. Selfish to a fault."

"She has changed." Lying there on the stony ground, he wept. "Though she had no need to. In my eyes she was always perfect. I live for her."

"And die for her once more. Foolish hound."

"The tie between us is still strong; it draws me on. But I lack the strength to rise."

For a long moment there was silence. True felt the

snowflakes melt against his cheek one by one. When the heat of his body faded, they would gather and cover him.

What would happen then to Barta?

"Hound, I have been more than merciful to you. It takes temerity to ask for more."

"Yes, Goddess."

"I tell you, however—in my mercy I will grant another boon. If you can get to your feet, I will grant you the strength to go on. But I do not think you will catch them. They are already far ahead."

True began to pant. Get to his feet unassisted? An impossibility. He could not see. The will that carried him so far had at last flagged; he tingled with weakness.

"Arise, True. Let us see of what you are made."

"Yes." If will would not serve, perhaps love would. He gritted his teeth and thought of Barta: the laughter that filled her face when they played together, the comfort of her presence. The sense of belonging he found in her arms when they lay together, when he gave her his seed.

The cord that connected them trembled. It pulled at him with a mighty force. His heart flailed in his chest.

He could not.

He must.

Arms trembling, palms fused to the cold ground, he pushed himself up. Somehow his legs moved beneath him; he knelt. Love and the desire for Barta's presence flooded him. From nowhere strength came.

Shaking in every limb he hauled himself to his feet. Vision clearing, he gazed into the goddess's silver eyes.

"Thank you, Mistress."

"I did not accomplish that. You did. Loyal hound!

Very well, I will grant you the strength to run on. I can but return the strength you had; I cannot grant more. I tell you with regret and in honor of your courage, I do not think you will be quick enough."

"I would be swifter as a hound."

"So you would, and gifted with far greater endurance."

"Then for her sake, I ask to be once more a hound."

"Do you realize what you say? What you request?"

"Yes."

"If I grant what you ask, if I change you back into what you once were, there can be no recourse from it. This will be the last favor you receive from me."

True trembled where he stood.

"Loyal hound, I can hear what is in your heart. Are you willing to live the rest of your life—short a time as that may be—as a beast, for her sake?"

"Anything for her sake."

"Bend your head."

He did, eyes closed, and felt the touch of her hand. There came a flash of light that reached through his eyelids, blinding, before he stood but shoulder high to the goddess and on four paws.

Without so much as waiting to thank her, he bounded off into the night.

Chapter Thirty-Three

Barta prayed for morning to arrive and put a finish to this endless night. Then it came to her—morning must long have dawned, yet the storm held the light at bay. They rode into fiercer weather rather than out of it, the intensity increasing as they went.

She did not see how True could possibly follow— how anyone could, especially on foot. Yet she could still feel him, and some short while ago the terrible pull of the cord that linked them had begun to slacken.

As if he drew nearer.

But how?

Now the pony faltered again—it needed another rest, but Barta did not think her captor would pause. Instead he tightened up on the reins and slowed the pace slightly.

He'd not spoken to her—not so much as a grunt— for some time. He must be as exhausted as she. Barta wondered if she should act while he remained distracted by the pony's condition and before they went any farther west. But the man's arm, like an iron bar, remained clamped across her midriff; his dirk now rode in a leather strap on the pony's neck, in easy reach of his hand.

What if Barta went for the dirk? Could she best him? Step after jogging step she contemplated it. Would she move swiftly enough? Her fingers, half frozen, might fail her. Then again, her captor's hands must also be chilled to the bone. Who was to say he'd move more quickly than she?

She thought of the man following behind them—of her love for him—and bared her teeth. Lifting her head in a sudden movement she let out a whoop that startled both man and pony, and went for the dirk.

The pony faltered and halted. The man swore, reached for the dirk also, and grasped it an instant before Barta's fingers closed on the hilt.

His hand knocked hers aside. He raised his arm, and she saw the blade coming at her, certain she would now die.

I am sorry, my love. I do not want for you to find me dead.

But the Gael's forearm, rather than the blade, caught her in a sweeping movement that knocked her from the back of the pony and took her to the ground.

She landed hard, and pain speared through her shoulder. For an instant, winded, she lay while her mind screamed at her to run. She scrambled up just as the Gael's boots came into her line of vision, telling her he'd dismounted. On her hands and knees she fled, crawling back the way they had come.

The cord between her and True glowed so brightly—felt so strong—she should have no trouble following it. Yet she heard the tramp of feet coming behind, far too swiftly. How many strides before her captor caught her? She struggled to her feet and ran.

****

Loyal panted, his tongue hanging nearly to the ground. A film of snow skittered beneath his paws, and the slash across his chest—which the goddess had failed to heal—still oozed blood slowly, a drop at a time.

But his lungs, now those of a hound, worked far more easily, garnering strength from deep breaths of air. And his heart once more beat steadily, deep and true, as if it gained might with every step nearer to Barta.

Now he knew she must be just ahead. He could feel it. And gladness possessed him, along with a hint of doubt.

Once more had he changed. Not only had the goddess transformed him back into a hound, but she'd left visible signs of enchantment. His great paws that reached for the ground were white—all of him, he saw, had become white as the snow that flew around him.

A gift of concealment, a boon to help lend surprise to the attack he planned? Loyal thought not. From Mistress Essa, he'd long ago learned white was the color of enchantment—animals who came from the otherworld appeared in that pure and ghostly hue.

The Lady had marked him. Not only had he changed from the man Barta had wed, but he no longer looked completely like her beloved Loyal either.

Would she know him?

Did it matter? His one aim in existing had now become delivering her from danger. Once more a single-minded hound, he could allow for nothing else.

But he'd run a great distance, for a long time, carrying a heavy wound. He could sense, if not discern, that dawn had broken behind him. Even his restored vitality began to flag.

How much farther could she be?

As if in answer he heard a scream just ahead,

uttered in a voice he knew.

Mistress.

Like an echo of her cry, his spirit returned the call. His paws reached farther, and new energy flowed from his heart. The blessed cord that bound him to Barta collapsed in on itself; just ahead he saw…

Two figures struggled toward him, one stumbling and only half upright, the other with a blade in his hand. Loyal's world snapped into focus. He forgot all want, all pain. With a bound, he leaped forward.

****

The great white hound erupted out of the snow as if formed from it, made into substance by some enchantment as wild as the storm around them.

Barta, stumbling forward at a hobble, suffused with pain, knew him at once despite the change. She knew him by the red slash angled across his deep chest—red on white, the colors of rarest magic—and by the feelings in her heart.

Staggering relief. Need answered, and love so profound it saw through any changes this world or the next might wreak.

Loyal.

She cried the word in her head, and for the merest instant his eyes met hers in a look that seared her to her soul. Then he hurtled past her—so close his white fur brushed her arm—and launched himself at the man who came hard behind.

The man with a dirk in his hand.

Barta spun, the breath seizing in her throat. She saw Loyal's paws strike the Gael in the center of the chest and take him down backward. Loyal stood on the man's torso and dove for his throat all in one magnificent movement.

Barta had seen Loyal do this before in battle—rend an opponent's throat or even his belly. For an instant she felt sure he must win now. He would vanquish the enemy, change back—somehow—into a man, her husband. They would go home, raise their fortress, and spend their lives together.

But this version of Loyal had run far, carrying a dire wound, and he did not move quite swiftly enough. Barta saw the Gael's dirk rise and fall, rise and fall, the blade flashing into and out of Loyal's ribs near his great heart.

She screamed and ran forward without thought or consideration for herself. Loyal had sacrificed his life for her once. He meant to do so again, but now one thing had changed.

His life had come to mean more to Barta than her own.

Willpower carried her forward, devotion fueled by sheer love.

She barreled into Loyal from the side and knocked him from the Gael's body, substituting her own where his had been. The Gael completed his stroke and the blade penetrated Barta's side, biting upward at an angle.

She felt the pain but distantly then. Determination—most murderous—held her in its grip. She seized the Gael by the neck, her hands like claws, and pounded his skull against the frozen ground—once, twice and again before, with a loud growl, Loyal pushed her aside in turn.

She fell back perforce as Loyal rent the Gael's throat. He turned next to face her, looking like a figure from a dream—white fur and hazel eyes gleaming, jaws dripping red and more red blooming at his heart.

He crawled into her arms with a whimper and sheltered there; she felt his great body shudder.

"Loyal," she whispered, "and True. By all that is holy, I know you now. Forgive me that I did not see the truth sooner." A sob wrenched her throat. "Forgive me for everything."

No response. Snow continued to drift down, lighting atop the red-stained fur, blotting out the wound. The hound's bright eyes had closed.

Did he breathe yet? She laid her hand over his heart. It beat, but low and slowly.

He would die here in her arms. After all he had done for her—endured and given—he deserved better, deserved more—warranted her life in place of his, if she could manage it.

She did not know how. The creature most beloved of her heart sprawled across her knees, the cord between them collapsed so she could no longer even feel it, while the life ebbed from him.

She buried her face in his fur, breathed in his scent—deep—and sobbed. Then she lifted her face to the sky and screamed: "Help me!" Prayer, incantation, demand. She vocalized every bit of love inside her, with Loyal's head cradled to her breast.

"Answer me! He deserves better than this."

What was it her mother had always said? Believe, for it to be so. Magic could not exist without belief. For an instant Essa's spirit floated at Barta's shoulder, put out a hand, and touched Loyal's white head.

"Mother, help me. Goddess, answer me! I will do anything, give anything, sacrifice anything."

Above Barta's head, the snow cleared. The icy

white orb of the moon appeared like a wise, milky eye examining her plight. The moon in daytime? What magic was this?

She could now barely feel Loyal's heart beating. Blood seeped from the wound in her side to mingle with his. Snow settled on his fur; she could scarcely imagine him rising.

But she must believe. Believe! In something greater than herself, greater than the world.

In their love and the connection that bound them spirit to spirit.

She closed her eyes and imagined her companion stirring, rising whole and strong—a man. When she opened her eyes once more, the shaft of moonlight had become a woman standing just beside her, over Loyal's body.

Beautiful she was, like the moonlight. And as cold? A beam of moonlight carries no heat, and this being's face bore no warmth. But her eyes—milk white as the moon itself—met Barta's, and she spoke softly.

"Brave hound."

Barta gulped back tears, her heart racing in her chest. "He is the finest hound—and man—ever to live. I know him now—"

"Too late. He is dying—again."

"You can heal his wound, if you will. My mother could have—"

"He perishes not from his wounds but from a burst heart. He ran too far."

Barta said without hesitation, "Then give him mine. You could do it if you chose. My heart still beats strong." By all that was holy, she could feel it pounding. "Pluck it from my chest, great goddess, and place it in his."

"And then, girl, you will die in his place."

"I do not care." Barta placed her cheek against Loyal's head. "Better that he should live than I—he is far finer and far more deserving. Gladly will I give you my life in trade for his."

"Ah." For the first time the Lady displayed some emotion. Her features smoothed in comprehension.

But she said, "Girl, I have already returned him to life from cold flesh once. What more will you ask of me?"

Desperate, Barta gazed up into the goddess's face. "A life for a life, only that."

The lady shook her head; her hair swirled around her like moonlight. She began to turn away.

And beneath Barta's splayed fingers, Loyal's heart ceased to beat.

Chapter Thirty-Four

The lady's radiance gathered in upon itself and swirled like mist about to dissipate. In a moment she'd be gone, leaving Barta there in the frigid dark with a dead hound in her arms. What could Barta say or do to make a difference? She'd offered all she had—all she was.

She threw back her head and wailed a single cry, "Love!"

For an instant the hovering moonlight wavered; then it continued to swirl. Barta closed her eyes in despair.

And heard a deep, male voice sound directly in front of her. "Hear her, wife. She speaks of love."

Barta's eyes flew open; they might just as well have remained shut, for she doubted what she saw.

The woman made of moonlight had once more coalesced. Another being stood beside her—tall he was, towering and glowing with dark green light. Half man, half stag, he emitted an aura of power as distinct as scent.

For a moment, Barta's heart seized in her chest. She would die here with Loyal, the two of them lying in the snow. Then the god looked at her. In his face Barta saw the compassion the lady lacked and such a strong force of life she had to blink.

The Lady answered him, "Do not interfere in this. I

raised him once. It is done."

"You raised him once," the god said, "and thus he remains your responsibility." Again his gaze moved over Loyal and Barta, tactile as a touch. "Did you not make him a promise? Yes, I heard what you said."

"What said I?"

"That if the girl knew him despite his changed form, they might remain together."

"I know him." Barta spoke swiftly, desperately. "I did not at first, but I do now. If this was the bargain…"

"So it was. And had he lived, girl, I would have held to my part of it and allowed him to stay with you. But he dies—again." The Lady turned a serene face to her lord. "It is finished."

For many long moments the two gazed at one another while Barta's desperation beat through her and she strove for something she might do or say to change the Lady's mind.

At last the Lord's voice rumbled, "Yet she speaks the word of magic: love. They love, wife, even as we love. They are as eternally bound."

The lady said nothing, but her gaze returned to Barta and Loyal, twined on the hard ground.

"I know their pain," the god went on softly. "Are you not lost to me each month? I am forced to watch you dwindle and slip away from me. Yet just when my spirit is darkest you reappear, and soon your lovely face shines full upon me once more. Then does my heart beat stronger and do I run more fiercely through the forest."

The Lady swayed toward him, pliable as a beam of moonlight.

"Do I not sing to you?" the Lord asked then. "Like

wind through the leaves, do I not cry out my heart and set the cords between us vibrating like music? Why should it be any different for these two? They are bonded. They love as we do. Should they too not be allowed to return to one another?"

The Lady sighed. "Love is eternal," she agreed. "As such, it will endure between them even if they be apart."

"In torment. Why do you think I cry songs to you if I do not long for you? Love was born when we entered the minds of the first beasts and men. The music is most ancient. Even I dare not still it."

"Nor I. But he has had two favors from me. I will grant no more."

Barta's heart sank. Already, Loyal's body cooled in her arms.

But the god spoke softly. "Yes—you granted the hound's request. The girl has had no gift from me."

He turned to Barta even as her heart rebounded sickeningly. He gazed at her with deep kindness.

"Girl, what would you ask? Speak the words carefully: they create your world and your future."

Barta's thoughts leaped, and she bade herself to caution. If she'd learned one thing since the night Loyal first died and she awoke to find herself lying beneath a sharp, deadly moon, it was the lesson of selflessness.

She gazed up into the god's broad face and spread her fingers on Loyal's fur.

"I want what he would want—no matter what it may cost me."

The god smiled. "Then let us awaken him and ask."

He bent and quite simply laid his hand on Loyal's head. Barta, reminded forcefully of her father's broad hand descending just so on the head of his hound more times than she could count, gulped back a rush of tears. Tenderness lay in that touch, kindness. *Love*.

Loyal's body jerked, and he stirred. Barta felt the bump against her knee as his heart started up, and the bright, warm surge as life filled him. The bonds between them—so still a moment ago—crackled.

The great white hound lifted his head, picking it up from Barta's lap. He gazed into her eyes. Bright hazel his were—those of the hound, the man, the spirit she loved.

Far more than the world.

Far more than herself.

Almost lazily he licked her cheek, placed his head against her chest and leaned in. She wrapped her arms around his head and let the tears come.

"Do not weep," the god admonished. "We are not done. Will you have him as hound or man?"

Barta shook her head. "I tell you—it is not up to me."

"Then we had better let him tell us, no?"

The god straightened. Loyal surged to his feet and turned to face him. For several moments they stood wondrously still; Barta sensed they communicated without words.

Radiance flashed, far brighter than the moonlight and many times more powerful. When Barta could once more see, she leaped to her feet.

The Lady had gone, faded like gossamer. The Lord remained, and in front of him stood a man—tall, lean and graceful as a hound.

"True?"

He turned and faced her. Naked he was, with a red

slash across his chest. His wheaten hair now bore streaks of white, but his eyes were the same. Bright and brimming with life, they contained her world.

Robbed of all speech, she reached out and seized his hands.

"Love is greater than we," the god said. "Remember that. The first thought before all others, it creates all we see, all we feel—all we are. Nothing can ever be more powerful." He smiled again. "Live in happiness, my children."

As simply as that, he slipped away into the gray dawn.

Barta fell forward into True's arms.

They wrapped around her, tight. The tears came again, but he swept them from her cheeks and kissed her, a kiss that felt like life returning. Joy flooded through her, making her tingle.

But she broke the kiss at last to ask, "Why? Why did you choose to be a man?"

"Ah then, Mistress, that is easy." He looked into her eyes and joy seized him also, uniting them. "Men live longer than hounds. It will give me more time with you."

Barta nodded, unable to speak. She summoned the frightened pony with a whistle, reproducing the Gael's signal as best she could. True donned the dead man's clothing—stiff with blood—against the cold. Together they mounted up and turned the pony's head back the way they had come—eastward into the new dawn.

Chapter Thirty-Five

True awoke when the sunlight touched his cheek, not before. He lay for the span of many heartbeats with his eyes closed, just sensing the day and experiencing his gratitude. Good to feel his heart beating. Good also to be a man once more and to know—because he could feel her—that Barta sat beside him.

Waiting for him to wake. She'd told him over and over again all he needed in order to mend was plenty of rest. Time. She would wait as long as it took.

So he lay there a few moments longer examining his condition. A man—no longer a hound, not ever. A husband with a wife who gladly—even joyously—deferred to him. New, that. Used to following her always, he couldn't quite get used to her waiting on him quietly as she did now. He might never get used to it. Then again, he might.

Gratitude knew no conditions—no more or less. Neither did love. Neither, as he knew, did belonging. They were absolutes. It did not matter who waited on whom, who bowed to whose will. Love had returned him to life; love was all.

Through every change, the love between him and Barta had never died, never flagged, never wavered.

Eyes still closed, he put out his hand. She slid hers into it. Pleasure suffused him. As easy—and as profound—as that.

He opened his eyes and looked at Barta. Gratitude mixed with the pleasure and flooded him again.

How beautiful was she, his woman. His friend. The other half of his spirit. Eyes of smoke gray seemed to contain the essence of the magic that had raised him. She'd braided her hair in an effort to keep it neat, but it gleamed warm red-brown as if it had trapped the light of autumn. At the front of her tunic he saw the swell of one small breast; he wanted to nuzzle into it, longed to nuzzle into her so much it hurt.

But that could wait. They had forever, as the great god had told him. Life after life after life.

She smiled at him, and he saw the beauty of her spirit shine.

"How do you feel, Husband?"

"Very well, Wife." He stretched luxuriously. "You let me sleep over-long."

"You need…"

"Yes, I know."

He needed something else as well. Three days had passed since they'd returned on their stolen pony. In that time they'd not made love, but now he rose for her like the morning sun.

"Wicked hound," she said with great affection. More than half the time she could read his mind. "Have you no shame?"

"What is shame? I love you."

"And I, you." She bent down and kissed him, a lingering caress of tongue on tongue. "But there's work to be done."

Yes indeed. The Epidii had taken back their former camp where so many—including Barta's parents and True's mother—had died. They'd gleaned anything useful from the Gaels' possessions and burned the rest in an act of purification. Now they concentrated on digging in.

Most of the wintering Gaels had died in that last confrontation. A few like the yellow-haired leader had fled. Sacred ground, once purified, would become sacred again.

Barta ran her fingers through True's hair. "You are very handsome, husband, with your streaks of white. Marks of honor these are—and of bravery. Here was I thinking you could not get more beautiful."

"I thought you said there's work to be done."

"Yes."

"But if you look at me that way, I will drag you off into the trees and take my pleasure."

"Will you, then?"

"Oh, yes."

Sadly she shook her head. "Not until that wound of yours heals. If you think I will endanger you again…"

He laughed. "But I heal swiftly—like a hound."

She caressed his bandaged chest with the lightest touch and sobered abruptly. "You have no idea how frightened I was. I almost lost you for the second time."

"No fear of that. You must let me show you my…"

He broke off when a cry split the air, a voice that sounded like Tally's calling Barta's name. She leaped to her feet and True followed, their fingers linking without conscious intention.

A mild day for the beginning of winter; now at midday a blessing of sunlight bathed the settlement. It showed True a party newly arrived, being greeted by Tally, Brude, and a number of other tribe members.

Strangers? Mostly. But surely he, True, knew one

among them.

"Wick!" Barta squealed at that moment. She drew her fingers from True's and ran.

Following more slowly, True stood and watched as Barta threw herself into Wick's arms. She and her brother both wept and laughed—True felt something inside Barta ease for the first time since Wick's departure.

Tally, his eyes also full of tears, turned and smiled at True. "I told you. Now everything will come right."

****

"We had no end of difficulty finding you," Wick confessed. He buried his face in his mug of heather ale, included among the supplies he and his party had brought with them. "No way to tell where you would be. Then I said to Verica, 'We will try the old place. A miracle may have occurred and they have retaken it.' "

Verica. Barta turned her gaze on the woman who sat, mostly silent, at Wick's side. A high-ranking member of the tribe Caerena she was, whence Wick had gone when he left the Epidii. The widow of their war chief, she appeared to be half warrior herself—like Barta—but beautiful with it. Long black hair cloaked her shoulders, and fierce blue eyes regarded the world from a finely sculpted face.

Just what lay between her and Wick? Barta could not say, but she felt something significant linking them. She had come, so Wick said, with the intention of joining forces—Epidii and Caerena—to make a united stand against the westerners, come spring.

Barta sensed far more. Would they unite the two tribes through marriage?

Tally, sitting on Barta's other hand, smiled. They'd

all met round the fire to discuss plans, Barta and True, Tally and Rekka, even Brude, with an unaccountably silent Avinda at his side.

Brude spoke now. "Do you, Wick map Radoc, intend to take back the place of chief?"

"I do." New steadiness inhabited Wick's voice and certainty filled his eyes. He looked sure of himself—at peace. He glanced at Verica. "We do."

Barta's eyebrows lifted. Well, that clarified matters.

Wick, looking at Brude, went on, "Not to say but I owe you more than I can ever repay. Thank you for stepping in when I did not see my way, and helping my family keep the tribe together. I hope we are still friends."

Brude hesitated. He too slanted a look at the woman who sat beside him before extending his hand to Wick. "Friends."

The two men clasped arms. True saw Barta blink rapidly as tears flooded her eyes.

"Together," Wick said, sounding very like his mother, "we are far stronger than ever we can be apart."

"Together," Tally chimed in, "we will build something that will endure."

To Wick, Barta said, "How did you and Mistress Verica meet?"

A curious smile crossed Wick's face. "How best to answer that? When I left our tribe, I thought I fled the unbearable pain that lay here. Cowardly, but yes—I do not try to hide what I am. I told myself I went to enlist the help of Father's old allies in our fight.

"Instead I believe I was led. I went astray in a storm, nearly stumbled on yet another party of Gaels, and realized I was too far west. When I turned back, I came upon the Caerena lands."

He glanced again at Verica, who took up the tale in a smoky voice. "We, like you, have been dug in, resisting the Gaels, far too long. The party Wick nearly encountered had just delivered a killing blow—over the last year our chief, war chief, and most of our warriors have been slain. It will tell much of how far we'd sunk that I—widow of the former war chief—held the reins in my hands. There was no one else."

Softly Wick said, "After I arrived, Verica and I spoke long. Father never had close ties with the Caerena. I cannot imagine why."

"We were originally located much farther west," Verica remembered. "Many other tribes have been displaced." She smiled at Wick. "It was chance that we met—or yes, you were led."

"Led," he concurred, a tender note in his voice that told Barta much.

"Be that as it may..." Verica lifted her head. "It seemed more than apparent we should join forces if it be to your liking. I and the men I've brought are but the vanguard. The rest of my folk follow. Together we shall stand or fall."

"Stand," Brude decided surprisingly. "Winter is the time for weddings. Avinda and I wanted to announce that we will wed." His gaze met Wick's. "What of the two of you?"

Verica smiled into Wick's eyes before reaching out and taking his hand. "There is strength in union. And I would be honored to become this man's wife."

Wick raised her fingers to his lips. "The honor will be all mine."

"So might it be," Tally said gravely, speaking for Radoc and Essa, and all those who had come before. "Caledonian hearts, as we know full well, are loyal and true."

****

The fire had died and night had come again. The settlement, bustling all day with activity, voices, and even laughter, had at last begun to quiet. Barta, daughter of Radoc, lay in her husband's arms hazy with contentment, and gazed up at the moon.

A sharp wedge it was, heralding new beginnings. Strange how the moon came and went, constant in its inconstancy. But the love never wavered.

"It is remarkable," she murmured to her husband. "If I keep my eyes on the moon and do not look at you, I can't really tell who you are."

"You know who I am," he returned.

"Yes, but you understand what I mean. You might be True. You might be Loyal. A hound or a man."

"Yes, but either way I am me."

"This is so." Joy bubbled up through her.

"I am he who loves you. Does it matter how I appear? What skin I wear? Barta, look at me."

"Not just yet. I would enjoy the moment."

"Look at me."

The corners of her mouth turned up. "Giving me orders now, are you?"

"Yes."

"My, how things have changed."

"That is just my point. Nothing has changed. Nothing ever will."

Barta turned her head and looked at him. She fell into the bottomless love in his eyes.

"Give me all the orders you like," she told him breathlessly.

"There is but one: love me forever."

"Yes," she whispered against his lips. "Bound spirit to spirit, forever and always. Because, as my brother says, Caledonian hearts are loyal and true."

A word about the author...

Award-winning author Laura Strickland delights in time-traveling to the past and searching out settings for her books, be they Historical Romance, Steampunk, or something in between. Author of numerous historical and contemporary romances, she is the creator of the Buffalo Steampunk Adventure Series set in her native city. *Loyal and True* is the first book in her new historical Hearts of Caledonia series.

Born and raised in Western New York, she's pursued lifelong interests in lore, legend, magic, and music, all reflected in her writing. Although she enjoys travel, she's usually happiest at home not far from Lake Ontario, with her husband and her "fur" child, a rescue dog.

Thank you for purchasing
this publication of The Wild Rose Press, Inc.

If you enjoyed the story, we would appreciate your
letting others know by leaving a review.

For other wonderful stories,
please visit our on-line bookstore at
www.thewildrosepress.com.

For questions or more information
contact us at
info@thewildrosepress.com.

The Wild Rose Press, Inc.
www.thewildrosepress.com

Stay current with The Wild Rose Press, Inc.

Like us on Facebook

https://www.facebook.com/TheWildRosePress

And Follow us on Twitter
https://twitter.com/WildRosePress